The Ones Who Stayed

The Ones Who Stayed
Copyright © 2025 by Melissa Agawa

Published in the United States by: Breakwater Press & Melissa Agawa
All rights reserved. No part of this book may be reproduced by any mechanical, photographic, or electronic process, or in the form of a phonographic recording; nor may it be stored in a retrieval system, transmitted, or otherwise copied for public or private use - other than for "fair use" as brief quotations embodied in articles and reviews - without prior written permission of the publisher.

ISBN: 979-8-218-68888-2

First Printing, 2025

Printed in the United States of America

The Ones Who Stayed

Melissa Agawa

For Teagan & Alex,
Who taught me how to stay soft in a world that asked for armor. You are the wild joy and deep roots of my life.

And, for those who have held me, fed me, and believed in me in quiet ways, in fierce ways, in ways I'll never forget. This story carries your fingerprints in every line.

CONTENTS

- HOW TO BEGIN AGAIN — 1
- HOW TO SAY YES SOFTLY — 7
- HOW TO TEND A FIRE — 13
- HOW TO INHERIT A LIFE — 20
- HOW TO LET GO — 28
- HOW TO CARRY A CHILD — 33
- HOW TO LOCK A DOOR — 39
- HOW TO LEAVE A LEGACY — 46
- HOW TO DO SOMETHING SMALL — 53
- HOW TO KEEP BREATHING — 61
- HOW TO SIT WITH THE DYING — 70
- HOW TO SIT IN A CIRCLE — 76
- HOW TO PLANT A TREE — 82
- HOW TO STAND FOR SOMETHING — 87
- HOW TO GET A JOB — 93

| HOW TO SHINE ON 99
| HOW TO LISTEN WHEN IT'S QUIET 106
| HOW TO LOVE 112
| HOW TO LEAVE 117
| HOW TO STAY 122

HOW TO BEGIN AGAIN

She worked the grinder slowly, deliberately— nug by nug, each dense pallet of green pulled apart by her careful fingers. The metal teeth clicked and shifted; each turn, crumbling stubborn resistance into something softer, more willing.

On the table beside her, a chipped ceramic tray waited, sprinkled already with a few loose threads of leaf and a stray stem - the beginnings of something ritual.

The afternoon had that soft, sideways light that made everything look a little dustier, a little older, a little more beautiful. She didn't rush. She didn't check her phone. There was music spinning somewhere behind her — not loud, not demanding — just filling up the quiet spaces like steam from a kettle.

She licked her thumb, gathered the fluff from the grinder's rim, and padded it down into a neat pile. All the motions were muscle memory by now, same as brushing her teeth or tying her shoes. Simple tasks that slowed the world enough to climb inside for a minute.

Outside the open window, the trees breathed slow, the heavy green of late spring trembling just enough to let the sun through. She rolled the first joint, loose and forgiving, and set it aside. Rolled the second a little tighter. A third, a fourth. Not for a party. Not for anyone else, really. Just stocking up for the days ahead.

She had been practicing this thing lately: trying not to treat joy like it had to be deserved. Trying to treat it more like food, like air. Something simple and constant. Something she was already allowed to have.

It wasn't always like that. There was a time not so long ago when she'd scrubbed the sink before allowing herself to cry. When joy felt like dessert, only after the work was done, if she'd been good. Once, she'd skipped a night swim with friends because she hadn't vacuumed, then lay awake in bed with the sound of water still echoing in her chest, like the ghost of something she'd nearly touched. Back then, joy had felt like a locked garden – beautiful, distant, gated by guilt and unfinished tasks. Now she was learning to press her feet into the soil without asking permission. To taste the berry before rinsing it. To dance without tidying the room first.

There were bills on the counter. Laundry, she hadn't touched. A text she hadn't answered. But none of it was asking her for anything right now. Right now, it was just the quiet scraping of the grinder, the slow shuffle of paper and leaf, the gentle decision of which record to play next.

Right now, it was enough.

By the time the last joint was tucked into her little glass jar, the sun had shifted again, stretching its light in soft trails across the floorboards. She brushed the crumbs into her palm, tossed them into the breeze outside the window like a quiet offering. It felt good to give back something small.

Today wasn't heavy; today was for her people.

Lunch plans had already been set — a corner table at a sleepy little spot where the walls were covered in old concert posters and the iced tea tasted like it had been brewed in the sun. It was her dear friend Abigail's birthday, and Caleb would be there, too.

Caleb, who moved through the world like a rhythm you didn't know you'd been missing until you heard it again. He'd built his farmer foot drum years ago – just a salvaged crate and an old kick pedal – but even offstage, he carried that timing. He had a way of sensing the unspoken, passing you a drink before you realized you were thirsty, shifting closer when your laugh started to fade. He didn't ask for much. He just stayed steady, quiet, and luminous, like a full moon behind thin clouds. Not by accident, but not with announcement either, he'd be there simply in the sense that they all just *fit*.

She threw on a soft linen dress, the color of the river after rain, and left the house with a spring still hiding in her step.

By the time she got there, Abigail was already halfway through a laughing story, arms flying wildly, painting the air with her happiness. Around the table, a handful of friends leaned in, catching her energy like sparks on dry grass.

The booth was crowded, legs tangling, shoulders brushing, plates weaving a lazy orbit between them. Fried green tomatoes, sweet potato fries, shrimp and grits, black bean burgers — a little bit of everything, like a shared language they all spoke fluently.

And Caleb – he sat across from her, smile tugging at the corner of his mouth like he was in on some joke that hadn't been told yet. His fingers tapped lightly against his glass, not out of impatience, but in rhythm, like he was keeping time only he could hear. She met his gaze once, twice, each time feeling it hum through her chest like a soft bassline - steady, warm, unspoken. Not a thrill, exactly. More like a memory finding shape.

After dessert — chocolate lava cake and a messy candle, Abigail blew out with a dramatic gasp — they all drifted outside, blinking into the bright afternoon. Plans splintered naturally: some back to work, some off to breweries, some just wandering. She found herself walking with Caleb without ever having decided to. Just the two of them, steps falling into an easy, familiar rhythm.

The guitar shop was a happy accident, or maybe not.

The bell above the door jangled when they pushed it open, and the smell of wood and strings and ancient dust wrapped around them like an old song.

Caleb picked up a weathered acoustic, the grain of it like a riverbed, and tuned it with easy, calloused fingers. His hair curled slightly at the temples, like it always wanted to stay a little wild, and the corners of his eyes crinkled when he smiled – creases earned from laughter, not worry. He had that open-faced kind of handsomeness that snuck up on you, soft around the edges but quietly magnetic. His thumb bore a small crescent scar near the nail, the kind that comes from strings snapping back over time. He always tuned by ear – said it felt more honest that way. She leaned against a cracked leather stool nearby, watching and smiling with her whole body.

When he began to play, it wasn't showy. It wasn't for anyone but the song itself. Slow, thoughtful chords that seemed to find the right words even before she did.

Without thinking, she began to hum along, her voice barely a thread of sound, catching on to the melody like morning light on a spiderweb. And then, without really meaning to, the words spilled out:

The river doesn't ask where the ocean's been,
The roots don't beg the sky for rain,
The stone don't blame the river's bend,
And I don't need to know your pain — just stay, just stay...

Her voice was soft, a little shaky at first, but sweet — so sweet it tugged at the air between them. Caleb slowed the strum instinctively, the notes adjusting like they understood her. He played without looking, his fingers moving with that familiar ease, like the chords had lived in his hands for years. A stone pendant shifted softly against his chest as he moved, river-washed and dark, strung on worn leather. He finally looked up – just once – it wasn't dramatic. Just a flicker, a quiet lift of his eyes. But in them was something too tender to name.

Not possession. Not conquest. Just the simple astonishment of finding something true and holding still long enough to let it land.

When the song faded into the wood and air again, they didn't say much; didn't have to. She knew it the way you know a secret.

HOW TO SAY YES SOFTLY

The night was stitched together before it even began.

One of those rare nights you knew, somehow, would make a little permanent home inside you. Not because of anything huge—not because of grand adventures or breathless drama, but because the people were right, the timing was good, and the world felt briefly, quietly willing.

She slipped into a favorite pair of jeans — soft as paper, frayed a little at the knees — and layered a loose, off-the-shoulder sweater over them. Comfortable but just a little magnetic, like she was dressing for herself, first and foremost.

Abigail picked her up just after sunset, a faint nervousness on her face like she was wondering if they were doing it right. Abigail was always like that — so bright inside, but quieter about it. She never needed to be the loudest one in the room to feel at home.

Lila slid into the backseat a few minutes later, lip gloss shimmering, denim jacket covered in enamel pins, energy buzzing out of her as though every cell in her body was tuned to a radio station that no one else could hear. She talked fast, bright, alive — stories tumbling over one another, laughter spilling out of her before she could even finish her thoughts. Lila had the kind of heart that could flood a city if she ever let it. Hers was a heart sewn together with resilience, with all the deep blues and candy pinks of knowing exactly how high and how low love can go.

The bar was a second-story joint tucked between two buildings in the historic district of town. They climbed a set of narrow stairs, the music already reaching for them — a living thing. Inside, the band was halfway through a set, warm bass was thrumming the floorboards, and vocals wrapped all the way around them.

They found a corner by the window, ordered a round of cheap beers and fancier cocktails, and let themselves be pulled under the spell of a Friday night that asked for nothing but their presence.

Lila danced with strangers and sang along at the top of her lungs, dragging her into a shy two-step that dissolved them both into fits of giggles. Abigail stayed close to their booth most of the night, a gentle anchor amid the wild spinning of the room.

Somewhere between songs, her phone buzzed. She checked it without much expectation, thumb half-smeared with condensation from her glass, and froze, smiling before she even realized she was smiling. A text from Eli. Just his name on the screen felt like an inhalation.

He never sent many words, but the ones he chose always landed gently, like stones placed just right to cross a stream.

> *Hey… I've been meaning to reach out. Things have been wild with the kids lately. But I keep thinking about you. Dinner again sometime soon? You're special. I don't want to lose the chance to know you better.*

Her heart softened in her chest.

Eli, with his slow smile, his hands that moved like he was fixing something invisible in the air, his quiet way of seeing people without rushing them.

She remembered how, at dinner, he'd folded his napkin into a neat square before they left, smoothing the creases like it mattered. It hadn't been anything flashy. Just a booth, warm food, and conversation that stayed with her longer than she'd expected it to. There was something in him, a steadiness, a thoughtfulness that called to her like water calls to stones. Not loud. Just inevitable.

She understood, more than most, how life could pull you in all directions when you were raising little lives. She understood the exhaustion, the constant shifting of priorities, the weight of carrying small worlds in your arms every day. A soft, patient affection welled up in her. No urgency. No bitterness. Just a gentle yes, blooming in her chest like the opening notes of a song she already knew by heart.

She tucked her phone back into her pocket, cheeks warmed more from feeling seen than from the beer. Lila spun back to the table just then, her hair messy, laughing loudly. Abigail leaned in with a mock-serious look, nudging her gently with an elbow. No questions, no teasing. Just the quiet kind of knowing you only earn from years of growing up alongside someone. She playfully rolled her eyes and smiled, "He's sweet," she said, affirming that her girlfriends knew her well.

The band rolled into a slow, swaying ballad. Outside the window, the town seemed to glitter against the night sky. They made their way home an hour later. Goodbyes were lazy, sprawling things — Lila hopped into a ride share with a cheery wave, Abigail driving off in her car with a sleepy grin and promises to text tomorrow. She went inside, home alone, windows open, the cool spring air thick with the smell of rain and lilacs.

When she finally slid into bed that night, the sky outside her window already dissolving into deep navy, she picked up her phone again. Her thumbs hesitated for just a moment, feeling the small, precious weight of choosing presence over pressure, and then she wrote:

> *I'd love that, Eli. Maybe something outside, if you're up for it? There's a trail I love out by the lake. I could pack a little picnic. No rush if you need to figure out timing with your kids. Just would be nice to see you.*

She hit send without second-guessing it, letting it float out into the night like a paper boat, trusting that if it was meant to reach him, it would.

He answered the next morning, early, before the sun had even cracked the sky wide open.

> *That sounds amazing. I'm free next Sunday. I'll bring the coffee if you bring that beautiful smile of yours.*

She laughed under her breath, burying her face in the pillow for a moment, savoring the warmth in her chest. It wasn't about swooning or breathless romance. It was about being seen and about choosing to see back. It was about letting life open at its own gentle pace, like wildflowers along the edge of the dunes.

She thought about the trail she had in mind — a winding path through old pines and soft beds of needles, a secret place where the woods opened suddenly into a bluff of golden grass, and then there was the lake, stretched out endlessly and holy in front of you.

Lake Michigan. Breathing and alive.

A body of water so vast it cradled storms, held moonlight, whispered the names of the lost and the found. She had always loved it like a sister. She'd always felt the feminine energy humming under its shifting surface — wild and nurturing, patient and feral, like something that could hold all her broken pieces without ever asking her to be smaller than she was. It wasn't just water.

It was a memory.

It was a promise.

It was prayer.

Next Sunday. A walk in the woods. The sun on her skin, the salt kiss of the air, and a new conversation waiting to be born.

She closed her eyes, her hand resting lightly over her heart, and made a small, silent vow: to move slowly, to stay open, to trust the earth to catch her, the way it always had, every time she was willing to fall.

HOW TO TEND A FIRE

The fire crackled low and steady, a stitched seam of sound against the cool spring air. She squatted by the edge of the small above-ground pit, her fingers feeding slender branches into the heart of the flames. The wood hissed and popped; each new offering swallowed into the slow breathing core. Her bare toes pressed into the damp, forgiving soil. The ground was cold, still waking up from the thaw, but there was comfort in the chill and a reminder that she was here, breathing and alive.

Each breath came slow and full, carrying the scent of woodsmoke, wet earth, and the faint, bitter sweetness of spring's early pollen. She continued to feed slender branches into the flames, watching them blacken and coil inward, releasing. The fire hungrily accepted every offering — broken limbs, fallen brush, shards of an old bed frame she'd chopped into manageable lengths.

Around her, the backyard was a patchwork of thaw and debris – broken limbs, scattered brush, pieces of a winter too heavy to hold itself upright. The storm had left her world ragged, littered with splinters and wreckage, but the sun had returned afterward unapologetic and golden. When it hit the ice-encased trees, the whole town had glittered like a cathedral made of glass.

She remembered the dark days of the storm, though, as she collected its remnants for the fire. She and so many others would long remember those long days spent silent and shivering in the dark. There were no lights humming in the distance. No TV static. No phone calls, just candlelight and the sound of the earth settling itself under a heavy shell. She had never known a silence like it. Not loneliness, not quiet. It seemed more like a suspension, a breath between worlds. It was strange how easy it was to burn the past when it had already broken itself apart. The smoke rose lazily into the evening, sweet and biting at once – part ash, part memory.

She shifted her weight, feeling the mud give slightly beneath her heels. The sensation grounded her, not just to the earth, but to herself. The rough edge of bark in her palm, the sharp crack and hiss as the wood surrendered to flame, and the rhythmic creak of the tire swing behind her, cutting through the soft roar of the fire.

Maggie spun slowly in the tire swing, hair catching the light, arms thrown wide like a bird mid-flight. Her laughter lilted across the yard, weaving into the smoke and ash, stitching the morning into something tender and alive. "Look, Mama!" Maggie called, her voice bright and holy against the roughness of the world, "I'm flying and spinning and rooted all at once!"

The words landed heavy and sweet in her chest. *Flying. Spinning. Rooted. All at once.*

She smiled, shifting another cracked limb into the fire. The flames caught it greedily, unfurling smoke toward the bruised-blue sky. Her mind wandered, but it never drifted far, always tethered by the feel of her feet on the earth, the weight of the air, the smoke rising like small prayers. Yet, memory found its way in, as it always did when she tended fires. Memory, like smoke, knew how to slip through the smallest cracks.

She thought of Jonah. She had met him long before she knew he would matter. How strange it had been, seeing him again after all those years. How familiar his face had looked, older and rougher around the edges, but still carrying an unforgettable gentleness.

Back then, when they first met at the bar, he would wait for Mae to finish her shift, while she was pouring beers and mixing cocktails with hands still clumsy from youth. It had been nothing but easy conversation, small smiles, glances that stretched too long but meant nothing yet.

It had been years later, long after Mae had died — an accident, sudden and brutal, like a page ripped out mid-sentence — that he resurfaced on a dating app. She knew deep down that this had all been more than a chance swipe of a familiar name blinking on her screen like some sort of forgotten song humming back to life.

They met again on a quiet, rainy afternoon that smelled like goodbye from the beginning. They sat on her backsteps drinking coffee neither of them wanted, talking about the places they'd been scraped and stitched since the last time they crossed paths.

He told her about Eleanor, the woman he had proposed to and had loved with everything he had left. Eleanor had come into his life a decade after he and Mae had broken up. He shared with her how Eleanor had fought invisible wars during their time together, and how one night, she slipped too deep into that war and didn't come back.

He spoke quietly with words as delicate as blown glass, and she listened the way only someone who had carried unspeakable losses could. She thought about the ones she had lost, too — the ones she didn't talk about, like Rowan. He was always with her, living in her chest like an old song she only dared hum when the world was very, very quiet.

That night with Jonah, the conversation dissolved into something softer. Something that didn't need words. Their bodies found each other the way rivers find the ocean, inevitably, naturally, achingly. It wasn't just desire. It was recognition. It was permission.

Later, when he had to leave, he'd kissed her like he didn't know how to stop. Her lips had felt like magnets against his, too, but eventually she let him go, knowing that loving someone sometimes showed up in supporting them in keeping promises they've made to themselves.

The next morning, the ice storm came. It dropped her whole world into silence and glass. Power lines sagged and snapped. Trees shattered under the weight. Roads disappeared beneath frozen oceans of white. They texted when they could, quick check-ins when the cell towers cooperated.

Promised they'd meet again when the thaw came.

But the thaw came, and so did the silences, space stretched between their words. Until finally — a quiet, apologetic goodbye.

> *You're magic,* he wrote. *But I'm still trying to find my way home to myself – I am so sorry I thought that I was ready for "us."*

She'd never answered. There was nothing to say that wouldn't break them both open again. Some kinds of love were meant to be held like smoke.

Cupped gently.

Grieved without bitterness.

Released with prayer.

A sharp crack from the fire pulled her back.

She blinked into the present, grounding herself again in the feel of the dirt under her feet, the weight of Maggie's laughter rising behind her. Maggie had twisted the swing into a tight spiral and now spun wildly, a blur of color and light. When she finally staggered to a stop, dizzy and breathless, she tumbled toward her mother in an ungraceful, perfect heap of joy. She caught her effortlessly, arms wrapping around the small, solid warmth of her and the smudged softness of Mr. Bunz, clutched tight in one hand. Once plush and white, he was now the color of the woods and garden, with accents of smeared magic markers here and there, one ear slightly askew, fur thinning in patches. Maggie loved him sometimes, most – equal parts pillow, protector, and co-conspirator.

Magnolia – wild blossom blooming under a wide, complicated sky.

"Mama," Maggie said, voice half-lost in her shoulder, "Do you think when we miss people really, really hard... they can feel it? Like a little hug inside them?"

The fire popped again, sending a spiral of sparks up into the endless blue. Her throat tightened for a moment, the weight of every goodbye she had ever carried pressed against her ribs. She closed her eyes.

Then, slowly, she pulled Maggie closer, breathing in the wild scent of her hair, and feeling the soft thud of Maggie's heart against her ribs - the steady pulse of life pushing forward, despite everything.

"I think they do, baby," she whispered. "I think we're all little embers from the same big fire. And when we love someone... even when we miss them... our embers glow a little brighter. Maybe that's how they find their way back to us," she smiled, "What do you think?"

Maggie nodded, solemn and satisfied, like she was already a priestess of some truth too big for grown-up words.

The fire roared higher as she fed another limb into its heart. The earth warmed under their feet. The smoke wrapped around them in slow, silver arms. And she thought, not for the first time, that survival wasn't about dodging the fires. It was about tending to them. It was about loving fiercely and letting go anyway. It was about spinning and flying and rooting all at once.

She kissed the crown of Maggie's head as she breathed in her wildness. Together, they turned back to the fire. Together, they kept it burning.

HOW TO INHERIT A LIFE

The house was quiet, breathing its slow, night rhythm. The Marantz spun low in the corner, some old folk record she barely remembered putting on – just soft chords and the scratch of time, threading through the room like low tide.

She sat at the kitchen table, bare feet tucked under her, papers spread out around her like fallen leaves. A cooling mug of coffee rested near her elbow; she'd forgotten it hours ago.

The estate case was heavy, not in volume but in weight. An artist–beloved, stubborn, dying–had asked for her help in ensuring her paintings would find their way home when she no longer could. Her client, the artist, had no vast fortune to divide, no bitter heirs fighting tooth and nail, just a dozen canvases, a few pieces of jewelry, a battered upright piano that still carried the fingerprints of a lifetime. She wanted them to be loved after she was gone. Wanted her small, beautiful life to ripple outward instead of vanishing.

She skimmed the draft again – clear, meticulous, kind.

The way she tried to be.

The way she hoped the world could be if tended carefully enough.

From upstairs, she heard the faintest creak of wood. She paused – *Was it Maggie shifting in bed, or maybe Connor tucking her in again?* She heard the low murmur of his voice, warm and easy, reading some ridiculous bedtime story they'd made up together the week before. A story about talking pine cones and a sassy raccoon. *Outlandish*, she thought, *but also adorable*.

The sound of it – his voice threading through the floorboards – settled her in a way she couldn't explain.

She smiled, without meaning to. Connor seemed to fit into the house like a breath she hadn't realized she'd been holding. Not living there, not woven in permanently, but near enough to be real, like a coat hung on the back of the door, or a mug always left out to dry. Familiar and trusted.

Near enough that Maggie asked for him sometimes, in that casual, trusting way children do when they sense someone would catch them if they fell.

She tapped her pen absently against the stack of paperwork.

The numbers blurred.

The words stretched and curled.

And before she could stop herself, her mind drifted – not far, not fast, but deep.

Sandalwood. The low clink of ceramic mugs. The old couch with fabric that scratched the backs of her thighs in the summer. She remembered an afternoon, years ago, before Maggie. Before college had ground the rough edges off her.

Sitting with her mother in the living room, a rare and tentative peace between them. The windows were open, letting the sounds of the neighborhood slip in – lawn mowers, kids shrieking, the distant thud of a basketball against the asphalt. Her mother had made coffee, strong and black, the way her father had drunk it. She poured her a cup without asking, the same way she did everything – brisk, efficient, unsentimental.

She remembered cradling the mug, feeling the heat bite into her palms, willing herself to think of something to say that would make the silence between them easier. Her mother reached for a book stacked on the coffee table – one of those old memory books, half falling apart at the spine. She opened it without looking, and a scrap of cloth slipped out – an embroidered square, frayed and yellowed with age. Small blue flowers were stitched clumsily around the name in faded thread, *Bluma*.

Her mother's voice had softened, just a little, barely enough to notice. "You bloomed the moment you opened your eyes," she said, almost to herself, "That's why we named you Bluma."

No other explanation.

No sweeping declarations of love.

Just that – a name, a memory, a tenderness so careful it almost didn't survive the air between them. Blue had nodded, swallowing the ache that rose sharply and sudden in her throat, tucked the cloth back into the book, and sipped the coffee, bitter and burning. She tried not to want more.

The papers in front of her blurred again. She blinked, pressing her palms flat against the table, feeling the grain of the wood bite back against her skin.

Connor's bare footsteps padded softly down the stairs; his hair was mussed from lying on Maggie's floor. He crossed the room without speaking, the faint scent of cedar and campfire trailing behind him – that smell she'd come to associate with his sweaters, his skin, his way of being close without crowding.

He set a hand lightly against the back of her neck, warm and present, and asking nothing. She let herself lean into the touch for a breath, just long enough to feel the grounding weight of it–before sitting up straighter, gathering the scattered pages into a neat pile.

Outside, the night leaned heavy against the windows. She signed her name at the bottom of the final document – her hand steady even when her heart wasn't. *Bluma...*

Inheritance.

Memory.

The wild, stubborn bloom of a life tended carefully against all odds.

She glanced once more at the file before closing it. Tucked the pen behind her ear, feeling the weight of the day slide off her shoulders in slow degrees. The work would still be there in the morning. It always was.

The lives she tried to tend, the stories she tried to honor – they would wait a few more hours for her, just this once. She gathered the papers into a neat stack, slipping them back into their folder with slow, deliberate hands, and yawned without meaning to.

Her body ached in that quiet, satisfying way that came from showing up for others, for herself, and for the life she was still learning how to live. She padded softly through the house, her bare feet against the cool floors as she moved toward the soft hiss and crackle of the turntable. Gently, almost ceremonially, she lifted the needle, silencing the record with a soft sigh of finality. She slipped the vinyl into its sleeve, cradling it with both hands, and slid it back into its rightful place on the shelf.

Small acts of care.

Small promises kept.

Then, lighter now, and at Maggie's door, she paused, leaned in, barely pushing it open. Maggie was sprawling across the bed in a tangle of quilts, one arm flung dramatically above her head, her mouth slightly open in sleep. Blue smiled, stepping into the room just far enough to smooth the cover around her daughter's shoulders. She brushed a strand of her hair off Maggie's forehead and pressed a kiss there, breathing in the scent of salt and earth and dreams.

Magnolia, she thought, the name blooming silently behind her ribs, *Wild and rooted, just like you were always meant to be.* She lingered a moment longer, feeling the pulse of love so deep it almost hurt. Then, careful not to wake her, she closed the door to a soft click behind her.

Connor was waiting near the base of the stairs, hands in the pockets of his sweats, sleepy-eyed but smiling at her like she was still the most beautiful thing he'd ever seen.

She crossed the room without hurry, folded into his arms, and let her cheek rest against the warmth of his chest. His heartbeat was slow and steady, anchoring.

"Thank you," she whispered, meaning a hundred things at once. "For being here. For being patient. For knowing when not to ask."

He didn't speak – just tightened his arms around her, the way he always did when she said things that mattered, and he kissed the top of her head, his lips brushing through her hair like a benediction. Then leaned back slightly, grinning at her with that lopsided, teasing look he wore so well.

"You know you still have a pen stuck behind your ear, right?" he murmured, tapping it lightly with his finger. She laughed under her breath – the kind of laugh that cracked something open and let the light in. Of course she did. Of course, she was still carrying the day's weight like a half-forgotten badge. She plucked the pen free, tucking it into the folder under her arm with a small shake of her head.

Together they climbed the stairs, the house creaked around them, the night folding in like a quilt, the world holding steady.

In bed, Connor shifted beside her, already drifting – his breath deepening, body folding easily into sleep. She lay awake a little longer, tracing the soft shadows the moon cast across the ceiling. It wasn't dissatisfaction that stirred in her chest. It wasn't restlessness. It was just her nature – how her heart had always moved. Wide. Unanchored, but never adrift. Capable of holding more than one melody at a time.

Earlier, when she'd opened the nightstand drawer, she'd found a matchbook tucked inside – one of those plain cardboard ones from the diner. Inside in Connor's slanted, half-messy handwriting, he'd written, *For your fire. Or your tea. Or whatever needs lighting.*

No signature. No explanation. Just Connor, finding small ways to show up in quiet corners.

She thought briefly of Eli – the easy way he laughed, the careful way he listened, the slow, patient orbit he seemed to be making toward her without hurry. He never pushed. Just checked in now and then with messages that felt like open doors. Once, he'd folded a paper napkin into a perfect square while they talked, quiet hands, quiet mind. It had stayed with her.

She thought of Caleb – the music still lingering in the edges of her mind, the way his smile wrapped around entire afternoons without ever asking for more. He carried a kind of reverence with him, even in casual moments – the way he tuned his guitar without ever looking at it, like the strings lived in his chest. She could still picture the river-stone pendant resting against his shirt, worn smooth from years of closeness.

And Connor – here and now, solid and breathing steadily against her side. He was a warmth she hadn't known she needed until it was quietly offered. There was still the faint smell of cedar on his skin, and in the drawer beside her, the matchbook he'd left like a breadcrumb, just in case she needed fire or light or some small reminder that he was with her.

None of it felt conflicted. None of it felt wrong. It felt like walking through a wild field, hands brushing every flower that rose toward her, without needing to uproot a single one.

Love wasn't a ledger; it was a landscape, wide enough for everything that bloomed inside it. She closed her eyes, letting her breath fall into rhythm with the house, the night, the soft, stubborn hum of her own growing heart.

HOW TO LET GO

The air held that gray, in-between stillness – the kind that made the world feel suspended, like a breath held just under the tongue. The kind of day that looked like grief, even if it wasn't. The sky was pewter that morning, low and soft and not quite ready to decide whether to rain. She didn't mind. Overcast skies made her feel like the world was giving her a break from being too visible.

Will had suggested the walk. Not quite a date. Not quite not one.

Birchbend Creek flowed with the quiet self-assurance of something ancient and unconcerned. The moss was brighter here, greener than she remembered. Softening stone, dressing the ruins of fallen logs, tucking its comfort into every jagged edge. Blue had always loved that about moss. It didn't ask for much. It just softened things.

She parked at the head of Birchbend Loop, where Will was already waiting in the small gravel lot. He leaned against his car, water bottle in hand, eyes a little tired. He wore that soft flannel she liked, the one that smelled like cedar and old smoke - familiar.

They didn't hug. They hadn't really done that in a while.

Will had started toward the trail head with his water bottle in hand. "Pretty day for a walk," he began. "It's been a while since we've done anything that wasn't … complicated."

She nodded. "Walking's good."

The path opened ahead like a breath, damp and silent. The birches stood in their silver stillness, bare arms lifting toward the sky as if mid-prayer. Spring was in the bones of everything – green coiled like a promise just beneath the surface. They walked in easy silence for a while. Will commented on the shape of a twisted tree. Blue pointed out a burst of crocus stubbornly pushing through a patch of melting snow. These were the things they could always talk about – the safe ones. Nature. Music. Bits of myth. All the poetry that stayed polite.

But beneath it, something unsaid tugged at her ribs like a caught fish. The ache of always being almost. Of almost belonging. Of almost being named.

They let the silence stretch between them as they continued into the woods. The trail wound quietly, moss softening the edges of stone, the birch trees rising in the solemn communion above. Birchbend Creek whispered beside them – low, steady, unbothered. "I've always liked this place," Will said, hands in his jacket pockets. "It feels old. Like it remembers what we forget."

She nodded, but didn't speak.

They walked the way two people do when they've said too much in the past, and now they're afraid of saying the one thing that can't be taken back. They reached a small wooden bridge at the midpoint of the trail and stopped. The creek fanned out beneath them, its song steady and sure. The water below ran clear and cold, weaving its way between smooth stones like it was in no rush at all.

"I can't keep doing this," she said quietly. Not angry. Not sad. Just clear. Like she'd come to the middle of a maze and could finally see the walls.

Will didn't answer right away. He stared at the water, lips parted slightly, as if trying to find a version of the truth that didn't hurt. "I know," he finally said. "I think I've known for a while."

She swallowed hard, leaning into the railing, fingers tracing the grain of the wood. "I want to be loved out loud. I want to be the truth someone doesn't flinch from."

Will flinched – barely. "I never meant to hurt you." He stood beside her, close but not touching, "You know I care about you?"

"I do." Her voice was gentle, but it didn't soften the truth. She turned to him, soft but steady, "And that's the hardest part. Because this–whatever this has been–it doesn't feel like love that's allowed to grow. It feels like love with a lid on it. And I can't breathe in that."

He looked at her, and then, for the first time in weeks, she saw the old ache in his eyes. The one that had drawn her in from the beginning. The boy-lost-in-a-man's-body gaze that made her feel necessary. He nodded once. Slowly. His face was unreadable, but his eyes flicked with something like grief. "You've changed me, Blue," he said.

She smiled, just barely. "It helps to know you let me in at all."

A bird startled from a nearby branch, its wings scattering the stillness.

She turned away, blinking at the creek's current. "You said once we'd known each other a thousand lifetimes."

"I still believe that," he said, reaching into his coat pockets.

She exhaled, eyes tracing the way the water curved around a boulder and kept going. "Then maybe this one wasn't the one we were meant to stay in."

He stood still and drew his hands from his pockets, pulling out a smooth river stone, flat and warm-colored. He pressed it into her hand. "It reminded me of you," he began. "Soft edges. Still strong."

She thanked him, closing her fingers around it.

They didn't hug.

They didn't cry.

They just turned and walked back the way they had come, together, but no longer entangled.

The moss caught her steps like a prayer. The trees didn't judge. The creek, faithful as ever, just kept flowing forward. And, just before the trail narrowed again, she glanced sideways and thought: *Some loves arrive to awaken us. Some to dismantle us. And some, just to remind us we're still alive.*

HOW TO CARRY A CHILD

The tent was already aglow with the first honeyed stretch of daylight when she zipped it open, letting the hush of evening air and her daughter's laughter echo from somewhere beyond the trees. They were camped on the edge of the state park – just the two of them – with their hammocks slung between two tall pines and the lake breathing steadily not far below.

She walked barefoot through the soft pine needles, her hands brushing back the ferns that leaned curiously across the narrow trail. She found Maggie crouched low over a patch of mushrooms – bright orange ones that clung to a fallen log like scattered embers. Her curls caught the sun in golden ribbons. "Mama," Maggie whispered, serious as a botanist, "These are not for dinner. They're for looking only!"

She grinned, squatting beside her, "Noted, Professor Magnolia."

They spent the afternoon balancing on the mossy logs over the creek bed, arms outstretched, giggling as they wobbled and caught each other. Maggie found a perfect stick – long and crooked – and dubbed it her wizard staff. At the shore, they built a crooked castle of sand and stone, decorating it with gull feathers and an occasional shell. They named it the Kingdom of Wonder. Blue laughed as Maggie made up royal decrees: no bedtime on Saturdays, hugs before every meal, and mandatory puddle-jumping whenever it rained.

They wandered like that for hours, slow and open, never quite heading in any direction, barefoot, heads tipped back to watch the clouds. They filled their pockets with pebbles and feathers and a single fossil Maggie declared to be "at least a million hundred years old". Dinner was simple – fire-warmed soup from a thermos and a handful of berries they'd picked along the trail. The wind smelled of moss and lilac.

That night, after the fire had burned low, Maggie danced barefoot around the glowing embers with a hula hoop that pulsed with colored lights, twirling, spinning, a blur of laughter and neon ribbons under the stars. Blue clapped along, belly sore from smiling. They fell into the hammock together, still giggling, cheeks flushed and hair smelling like smoke and sun.

Later, curled up together in the hammock beneath a sky blooming with stars, Maggie pressed her cheek to her mother's collarbone and murmured, "I wish we could stay out here forever. Just me and you and the stars."

Blue kissed the top of her daughter's head. "We kind of are," she whispered. "This is forever right now." A hush followed – a sacred silence. The kind that invited memories in.

Maggie wasn't the first.

There had been a baby before her – a quiet life that never had the chance to speak. Blue had been twenty weeks along when they found out the baby was a boy. They'd named him Leighton. She had imagined his face, had folded his tiny clothes, had begun dreaming him into existence.

When it ended – suddenly, cruelly – it was as if the world had stopped. Dean was away on a business trip, and when she called to tell him, his voice had been strained, distracted, as if he were juggling something else. He didn't come back right away. He said, "I can't get out of this meeting."

The night she lost Leighton, she had held her belly alone in the emergency room, her body bleeding away the little life it had been building. Her body still made milk. The world spun forward without pause. There was no hand to hold, no forehead to kiss. Only fluorescent lights and a nurse who whispered, "I'm so sorry, sweetheart."

It was the beginning of the end. Dean had never been cruel–not exactly. But he had always made her feel like a burden when she needed something real. And when grief cracked her open, he was already miles away. She learned, quietly and without ceremony, how to carry it herself.

She hadn't known how to grieve that kind of absence at the time. She'd wandered her own house like a ghost.

And then, in time, Maggie.

That labor had felt like crossing a threshold carved in bone and moonlight. She labored at home with a midwife named Tova, a tall woman with a crown of silver-streaked curls, skin like cedar bark, and hands that smelled faintly of eucalyptus and sage. Tova moved like a tide, unhurried and vast. She wore long skirts and carried with her the scent of earth after rain. Her eyes were green, clear, steady – and when she looked at you, it felt like being seen by a forest. Tova barely spoke unless words mattered. Her hands held stories, firm and warm, and her eyes had that quiet shine of someone who had been through both too much and just enough.

At some point, she had wept – not from pain, but from the ancient flood of it all. "I don't know if I can do this," she'd whispered, knees pressing into the floor, forehead damp.

Tova had knelt beside her and said only, "You are already doing it. You were made to do it. You are a wild and holy storm."

Magnolia had come into the world just after dawn, her cry slicing the hush like birdsong. Blue remembered the feel of her – slippery and sacred, eyes not even open yet, and already knowing everything.

Her body had felt carved open not just physically, but cosmically. Every truth she'd ever held poured out with the blood and afterbirth.

She'd named her not for a family line, a saint, or a trend, but for a tree. A bloom. A promise. *Magnolia*. Soft and strong. Fragile and feral. Alive.

Dean had been there for the birth, at least physically. He stood behind Tova, watching like a man at a distance from a campfire – close enough to see the glow but not warmed by it. He had tears in his eyes when Maggie arrived, and kissed Blue's forehead like he meant it, but she could feel that the gap between them had already stretched too wide to close. He'd been scattered, gone more often than not. Sweet when he showed up, but never staying long enough to unpack the weight he carried – or the weight he caused.

Back in the hammock, Maggie shifted and looked up, "Mama?"

"Hmm?"

"Do you think trees remember things?" Maggie asked curiously.

Blue smiled, eyes still on the stars, "Yes, baby. I think they do."

"Even the sad things?"

"Especially the sad things"

"Even the things that they never got to say?"

Blue's throat caught a little. She kissed Maggie's cheek, "Even those," she whispered.

Maggie nodded, then yawned so hard her whole body lifted off the hammock for a second before flopping down again like a fish. "Goodnight, Mama," she murmured, already half asleep.

"Night, my girl."

The trees whispered overhead. The lake hummed its lullaby in the distance. And Blue lay still beneath the light of the stars, listening to the breath of her daughter, the rhythm of the earth, and the memory of a midwife's hand pressed to her back, steady and true.

In the dark, she mouthed a quiet thank you. To the daughter who had stayed. To the son who hadn't. To the woman she was still becoming.

And the forest, ancient and alive, whispered back.

HOW TO LOCK A DOOR

The house held its breath in the quiet way homes do when a child is gone for the night. No toys were left half-finished, no shoes kicked into corners, no low hum of a nighttime request whispered through the dark.

Just Blue, and the soft hush of space.

The house wasn't big – just two bedrooms, a single bath, and a sloping roof patched more than once with borrowed ladders and online tutorials. But it was stone, solid, and rooted into the earth like it had always meant to be here. A narrow creek ran behind it, winding through the trees, its voice constant and soothing like a heartbeat in the dark. This had been her first real home since the divorce. The first place she'd chosen for herself. The first place she and Maggie had ever planted anything new.

The windows were open, letting the dusk move through like a slow tide – cool and fragrant with pine and honeysuckle. Somewhere in the trees, a wood thrush sang its strange, fluted song, and the branches swayed like a lullaby.

She padded barefoot through the hallway, hips swaying to the rhythm of an old song playing from her phone on the sink – something she hadn't heard in years but knew by heart. Her underwear was mismatched, cotton and soft, and she wore nothing else but a laugh in her throat and the glow of the golden hour across her collarbones.

She danced.

Not for anyone. Not even for herself, really – but for the world. For the space. For the fact that no one needed her in that moment, and the floor belonged to her again. She twirled once, twice, arms loose above her head, and caught her reflection in the mirror – the bare skin of her stomach, the gentle dip of her waist, the crescent moons of old stretch marks she had long ago stopped calling flaws. Her body wasn't perfect, but it was something remarkable that had carried her here.

A blessing of blood and breath and bloom.

She laughed out loud then – loud enough to startle the dog – and caught the corners of the counter as she bent over, shaking her head.

And just like that, the moment shifted.

A truck roared past the house, engine too loud, tires spitting gravel. The dog growled low. Her body reacted before her mind did – eyes narrowing, breath catching, a flicker of something old and dark rising through her ribs.

She crossed to the front door.

Turned the lock.

Then the deadbolt.

Then again.

Then again.

The porch light was already on, but she checked the bulb anyway. Not out of fear, exactly. Just... habit. She moved through the rooms like muscle memory, making sure windows were latched, that the side gate was still chained, that the kitchen light stayed on. Her mind didn't speak in panicked words anymore. The danger wasn't recent. But it still whispered from somewhere deep.

Back in the bathroom, she dressed quickly – old jeans, soft at the knees, and a faded camisole with one strap stretched longer than the other. She smoothed her hands down her sides automatically, as if trying to press herself into someone smaller, less visible. Her eyes caught her reflection again. Just under her left rib, pale and puckered, the faint scar curved like a crooked smile.

It was nothing dramatic – a kitchen accident, she'd once told a date. But that wasn't true. Her eyes swelled – not from the pain of it, but from the way memory rose uninvited. That scar, that small knot of tissue, had felt like a brand for years. A reminder of everything she'd been told: that she was loud, that she was unlovable, that her body was too soft, too strange, too much.

And yet –

Her body had carried Maggie into the world. Had survived miscarriage and loss and sleepless years. This body had rebuilt a garden, shoveled snow alone, lifted a sleeping child into bed over and over again. Her body was a miracle.

She touched the scar lightly, not with shame, but with reverence. She was still here. Still whole, in all the ways that mattered.

She wasn't expecting Dean. She hadn't seen him in months. But that didn't mean her body knew how to relax. Back in the bathroom, she tried to laugh again, but the music had stopped. The moment had passed. She ran water over her hands, grounding herself in the temperature, the sound. She caught her own eyes in the mirror – clear, steady, tired.

A knock at the door.

Soft. Not the kind you flinch from.

Still, her shoulders tensed.

She crossed slowly, barefoot, one hand brushing the wooden edge of the hallway for balance.

Caleb stood on the porch, wind-tousled and earnest, holding a small bouquet of wildflowers – dandelions, yarrow, a sprig of lavender – wrapped clumsily in brown paper that looked like it had been torn from a grocery sack. In his other hand, a mason jar of herbal tea, still warm from the afternoon sun. He shifted his weight, scuffed one heel against the step like a boy about to apologize.

"I didn't know if you liked flowers," he said, eyes steady beneath brows knit in hope, "But I saw these and thought… well, I hoped maybe you had a vase."

"You still up for company?" he asked, "Or should I turn around and pretend I got lost on the way to my own kitchen?"

She smiled, soft but worn, "Come in," she said, and stepped back. "Just ignore the half-naked dancing ghost who may or may not live here," she smiled.

He grinned, "lucky ghost."

They sat cross-legged on the floor, the dog draped lazily between them, music playing low and scratchy from the speaker. Caleb didn't ask about the triple-lock ritual. Didn't mention the way her voice had wavered when she'd first opened the door.

He just poured her a cup of tea with the gentle precision of someone who'd learned not to startle grief, toasted to "Surviving the day," and told her a story about a baby raccoon he and another guy had rescued from behind the hardware store dumpster – a story full of awkward heroics and soft-hearted decisions, told with a smile that asked nothing of her but breath.

It was absurd. It was perfect.

She leaned her weight slightly against him, not quite touching, but close enough to feel his warmth. And when she reached across him for the mason jar, her camisole slipped again. His eyes caught on the curve of her rib, and the scar that lived there. He didn't flinch. Didn't ask. He just looked at her like he knew she could fold the moon into a paper crane if she wanted to. He reached out – gently, slowly – and traced the edge with his thumb, feather light. "This one looks like it tells the truth," he said quietly.

And she let out a breath she hadn't known she was holding.

They didn't need to speak about it. The body always remembers, but sometimes, so do kind hands. And later, when her breathing slowed, and she curled lightly toward him, not quite touching, he reached out and tugged the throw blanket up over her knees, anchoring it in place like a vow.

Not possession. Not seduction.

Just this, *You're safe*.

Outside, the stars had begun to shimmer above the tree line, one by one. The crickets sang their thousand-part hymn. Somewhere in the woods, a fox called once, sharp and brief.

She closed her eyes.

The creek whispered steadily beyond the house. And for the first time in a long time, the world felt like it wasn't watching her – it was holding her. And the house exhaled with her.

HOW TO LEAVE A LEGACY

The courthouse smelled exactly the same as it had years ago – a particular blend of old carpet, lemony floor cleaner, and the anxious sweat of too many lives colliding under its lights.

She tucked the folder under her arm, moving through the security line with the slow shuffle of a woman who had learned that nothing in bureaucratic spaces ever moved faster than it had to.

Today, at least, it wasn't about her. Today was Jack's day.

Jack – all charm and crow's feet and terrible Hawaiian shirts – was waiting upstairs with his coffee breath and his stubborn insistence on doing things *properly*. She smiled just thinking about him, stepping into the elevator with its scuffed walls and cracked vinyl flooring.

He'd called her two months ago, leaving a voicemail that began with, "Sweetheart, I need a will before the gold-diggers get it all," and had ended with something about a 1978 Dodge pickup he refused to let "the blonde one" inherit.

Didn't say who the blonde one was. Didn't need to.

Blue had known Jack for years, long before he started calling her sweetheart or bringing her seasonal pies he claimed he'd baked himself but definitely hadn't. He used to drop off handwritten notes scrawled on torn cardboard or napkins, with things like:

> *Need someone to make sense of my mess, and maybe tell me what happens to ghosts when their lawyers retire.*

She'd take them home like riddles. Like treasure maps.

He was in his seventies now – grizzled and sly, still calling her *kid* even though her knees cracked when she crouched. He had a heart condition, a fondness for cheap cigars, and a constitution immune to advice.

Not even Blue could tell him what to do.

When they'd sat down for their first official meeting about the will, he'd told her about his wife, Marianne, with a casualness that felt heavier than it sounded. She'd been sick for years.

How he'd loved her, steadfastly, until the very end.

And how grief hadn't come crashing in like a storm, but rather drifted in like an old friend, quiet and familiar.

And now, he said, grinning with no small amount of mischief, he was "outnumbered" again – this time by his own foolish impulses and a small army of twenty-something waitresses who winked too easily once the bingo pot swelled past fifty.

Blue liked him immediately. Not because he flirted shamelessly with every woman under sixty, but because under the bravado was a man who knew what it meant to lose and still chose to laugh anyway.

He lived the way people sometimes only dared after they'd survived something brutal: loud, messy, without apology.

The elevator bumped to a stop. She stepped out, smoothing the papers absently with one hand. The probate division smelled even worse than the lobby – like dust trapped in paperwork. Still, a warmth unfurled in her chest.

There had been a time when walking into this building meant something else entirely.

Back then, she hadn't carried folders filled with other people's worries, she'd carried her own: papers that dissolved a marriage, orders that barred one life from another, and signatures that felt more like exorcisms than contracts. She remembered sitting on a cracked vinyl chair in the hallway – her body so still it hurt, the low buzz of those same fluorescent lights drilling into her skull. The feeling of being erased, piece by piece, by a man who had once promised to love her.

She shook her head lightly, exhaling.

Today was different.

She was here on behalf of a man who had loved without cruelty, who had survived his losses without trying to make the world pay for them.

Jack was waiting at the end of the hall, perched like a gangly crow on a hard-backed bench. He spotted her and waved a file folder wildly overhead like a flag of surrender. "Counselor!" he boomed, loud enough to turn heads. "Did you bring the paper that'll save my soul?"

She laughed under her breath and crossed to him, "Only if the judge agrees your boat is a legitimate beneficiary," she said, handing him a fresh set of copies to review.

Jack grinned, leaning in with mock confidence.

"Blue, sweetheart, if that boat ain't more faithful than half the women I've met since Marianne passed, I'll eat my fishing hat!"

She snorted, trying not to smile too widely as a clerk gave them a scandalized look from behind the counter.

This was their rhythm – gentle teasing. Jack's endless theatrics and Blue's dry patience tucked beneath affection. The kind of bond you build slowly, in stories and letters and long pauses that don't need to be filled.

The hearing itself was blessedly short. The judge, a woman with kind eyes and no patience for nonsense, signed off on Jack's modest, lovingly ridiculous estate plan without much argument. Blue watched Jack nod solemnly when the lilac planting clause for Marianne was read aloud, and she saw the way his hands trembled slightly when he scrawled his name across the final page.

Afterward, Jack insisted on buying her coffee from a vending machine so ancient it probably predated the moon landing. They sat together on a cracked bench under a window that barely opened, sipping canned coffee beverages that tasted like nostalgia and metal.

"You know," said Jack, "People think when you lose someone, it guts you all at once, but the truth is it's like getting a hundred tiny paper cuts every day. Little ones you barely notice. Until one day, you're bleeding out, and you never even saw the knife."

Blue nodded, the words slipping under her skin like sunlight through water.

"But then," Jack added, "You get your ass up anyway. You fall in love with a boat. You fall in love with a can of bad coffee. Hell, you fall in love with a pretty lawyer who won't even look twice at your old ass." He winked, grinning with too many teeth, and she burst out laughing before she could stop herself.

"Sorry, Jack" she said, still smiling, "Clients are off-limits. And I don't date men who lie about pie."

"Smart girl," he said, raising his can in a mock toast, "Real smart girl."

They finished their coffee, their boots knocking lightly against the old tile floor. Jack wandered off toward the elevators, humming something she half-recognized.

She lingered.

It had been here, in this very building, beneath the same indifferent buzz of lights that she once sat, clutching a manila folder filled with photographs she hadn't even known existed. Private things, stolen things, her own skin turned into evidence.

She remembered the bone-deep chill that hadn't left her for months afterward – not from the air, but the kind that settles when the ground you trust gives out beneath you. And now, here she was – alive, laughing, filing love stories for stubborn old men who knew better than to leave kindness unsaid.

The courthouse still buzzed with a thousand low dramas: broken promises, broken families, broken hearts, but they couldn't touch her now, not the way they used to.

She reached into her bag, pulled out a small leather notebook she used for case notes and grocery lists and poems she didn't admit were poems.

She jotted down a line from something Jack had said – something about ghosts and librarians and pie.

She'd work it into a letter someday. Maybe a story. Maybe just keep it for herself. Because the older she got, the more she found herself measuring time not only in years, but in the people who had stayed.

Not the ones who showed up in the high tide – when everything was bright and easy - but the ones who stayed when things cracked. When the porch light burned out. When the dishes stayed in the sink for three days straight. People like Jack, with their ghost stories and their half-sour jokes. With their bourbon coffee and goodbyes that don't quite stick.

She breathed in the dusty, lemon-tinged air. She felt the folder lightly- the weight of Jack's small, stubborn legacy pressed warm against her side, and then she turned toward the door – toward the sunlight slanting through the wide glass atrium, toward the wide-open, unwritten afternoon.

The papers had been filed.

The past had been too.

And she was still standing, still laughing, still here.

HOW TO DO SOMETHING SMALL

The morning smelled like wet pine and fresh soap. A breeze stirred through the birches that lined the high school parking lot, their new spring leaves trembling like they hadn't decided yet whether to stay. She pulled into her usual spot in her dusty Subaru – the one with a cracked taillight and a peace sign sticker peeling just lightly at the edge – and turned off the engine. For a moment, she sat there, watching the light break slowly through the trees. It was the kind of light that arrived quietly, without ceremony. The kind that didn't need to be announced to be holy.

She stepped out of the car, stretching her back with a small groan. Her shirt – a soft, over-sized vintage tee the color of washed-out moss – clung to her a little in the dampness. It had a small, hand-stitched sun just over the shoulder. She wore it often on days she didn't want to think about her body. The denim shorts had been thrifted years ago and were fraying at the seams in a way she found comforting. She pulled her hair into a loose bun, letting the stray curls fall where they pleased.

"Hey," came a voice behind her – warm, familiar, low like a song she knew by heart.

Eli stood there, holding up two sponges like offerings, already soaked through a streak of water running down his collarbone into the faded collar of his shirt. Soap bubbles clung to the dark hair on his forearms, which were stronger and more weathered than she'd remembered.

She smiled without meaning to. Something about him always softened the armor she didn't intend to wear.

"Ready to scrub our way into sainthood?" he teased, his smile crooked, easy, the kind that made people lean in without realizing.

"I was born ready," she said, grabbing a bucket and following him toward the circle of volunteers already forming. They were gathered for the Silver Hollow Pines – the school's debate team had been in a rollover crash just two weeks earlier on their way home from a winter invitational a few hours away. The roads had iced, the van skidded, and the world had shifted. The coach, a teacher who'd been a part of Silver Holllow for decades, and had led the team had shielded three students with her own body. One boy was still in a coma, two others were learning to walk again. There had been no deaths, but no one in Silver Hollow would ever forget the moment the news broke. A quiet snow had been falling that night, and it hadn't felt beautiful at all.

Today though, the snow was gone, and half the town had shown up for the fundraising car wash. Teenagers with soaked pant legs waved handmade signs at passing cars, someone's uncle had set up a grill nearby, and donation jars rattled with every few steps, bills folded and wet.

She fell into rhythm with Eli at the far end of the line; they worked in companionable silence at first – soapy water splashing over their feet, the sun slowly warming their shoulders.

He was focused but unhurried, his movements practiced and calm. A man who seemed to approach most things – people, too – like a long drive through back roads. No rush.

At one point, as she leaned across the hood of a burgundy SUV, her shirt stretched tight across her lower back and Eli instinctively reached forward, tugging the hem down with two fingers and a gentleness that didn't ask for thanks.

She met his eyes briefly – a soft kind of gratitude passing between them as a breeze rose from the edge of the school grounds, thick with lilacs and cut grass. She closed her eyes and let it pass through her. "I like this," she said, not looking at him, "Just.. doing something small that matters."

Eli dipped his sponge into the bucket and wrung it out slowly, voice low and thoughtful. "I think those are the only things that ever really do."

A pause stretched between them. Comfortable.

He glanced at her sideways, "You going to the benefit show tonight?"

She nodded, "You?"

"If you are," he said with a smirk she found impossible to resist.

Her laugh was soft, "Then yes!"

Their hands brushed a few times as they moved around the next car, unhurried. At one point, Eli helped her untangle a stubborn hose, their fingers locking briefly in the wet coils of it – not urgent, just easy.

He looked at her, not expectantly, but fully, like she was the only thing in the frame.

It wasn't a grand romance – not today. But it was steadiness. It was being known without explanation. It was a breath shared without rush.

The water glimmered on the pavement like little bits of sky had fallen and shattered there. She stepped in one puddle barefoot and didn't move right away.

By the time the sun dipped below the lake, the town had gathered at the park. Strings of lights dangled between trees like constellations. The band shell at the far end of town was lit with amber bulbs and the warm hush of anticipation.

She arrived with a folded blanket under one arm, the fabric still faintly scented with lavender oil and lake air.

Eli was already there, standing at the back of the field – the kind of place chosen by someone who liked to witness without needing to be seen. He wore an old flannel rolled to the elbows, a cider in one hand, and that quiet way of being that didn't press or pull.

He handed her the drink. She handed him the blanket.

They didn't need to say anything.

Cedar Kin took the stage with no fanfare. Caleb barefoot, his jeans frayed at the cuff, guitar slung casually over one shoulder like it had always belonged there. Amy, in a sage-colored dress, her hair braided down her back. June on bass, serene and steady. Michah at the keyboard, already coaxing a quiet shimmer of sound into the air, like the first wind before a storm.

"This next one," Amy said, her voice carrying like wind through the trees, "was written with the help of someone we love very much."

Caleb didn't speak – just turned his head, eyes finding Blue's with a quiet gravity that said more than words. A look that landed like a stone in water – small, still, rippling outward.

Then the music began.

The keys trickled first, soft and clean like water over stones. The bass followed – not flashy, just present, holding. Caleb's guitar entered next, each note round and deliberate, the grain of the wood almost visible in the sound. He paired it with the subtle thud of his farmer foot drum – slow, grounding, like footsteps on sacred soil. Then Amy's voice – dusky and warm, carrying the lyrics as though she'd found them folded inside the land itself.

> *The river won't rush just to get to the sea*
> *It bends, it waits, it hums patiently*
> *The wild don't bloom just to make us believe*
> *They grow because growing is what they need.*
>
> *We are moss on the stones*
> *We are fire under rain*
> *We are hands that still hold*
> *Even carrying pain*
>
> *So, breathe with me here, where the light breaks slow*
> *Where the wind knows your name but has nowhere to go*
> *Love isn't a promise; it's a place we remain -*
> *The fire, the water, the whisper, the flame*

The sound didn't build – it deepened. The music moved like roots under the soil, quiet but insistent, threading its way into marrow. Caleb's foot kept rhythm with the earth, jaw slack with focus, the kind that made even stillness look like prayer. Amy's voice held it all like a bowl.

In the crowd, Blue sat beside Eli, their joined hands resting in the grass, quiet and reverent.

Across the field, Amy and Caleb leaned into each other in the final chorus – not in performance, but in stillness. A shared breath. A language without words. Amy smiled with the ease of someone who no longer needed to explain the love they carried –

Because here, no one had to.

Theirs was a love lived in plural – not fractured, not lesser. Just open.

Like a field after rain.

The song ended in a hush. A long breath of gratitude moved through the crowd. Then, applause like waves.

Blue didn't move right away.

She felt the steady presence of Eli beside her – not leaning in, not touching, just there.

And in that nearness, a charge of something deeper than attraction.

The electricity of being seen. Really seen – without having to explain a thing.

She thought of Connor, of Caleb and Amy – how he'd looked at her like she was a horizon and not a question, how they moved around each other like trees shaped by the same wind. She thought of the way love can ripple outward and remain whole. She understood now that love wasn't a story with one plot.

It was a song with many harmonies.

And tonight, every note rang clear.

HOW TO KEEP BREATHING

The day had buzzed and bloomed in a way early summer days sometimes do – too bright, too fast, as if the world itself was drunk on the nearness of freedom. She barely remembered the open house anymore.

Ezra, the one who always seemed like a lighthouse to the rest of them. He was the oldest, steady and sure, already leaning forward to whatever life came next. Their parents had organized a celebration honoring his graduation. A day full of clapping hands, plastic chairs sinking into the lawn, and cousins climbing over one another for cake. Her childhood home pulsed with life: music on the stereo, paper plates stacked high, half-empty bottles of water and soda sweating on the counter.

That evening, Rowan had stayed home when it came time to leave for dinner. "Homework," he said easily, not looking up from his textbook. Nothing about it had felt strange at the time – not the way he waved them off, not the half-full glass of orange juice sweating on the counter.

He was that kind of boy – steady, brilliant, golden in a way that didn't feel forced. Football jersey in the fall, honor cord in the spring. His laugh carried across every cafeteria, warm and effortless.

Rowan was the kind of boy who could throw a perfect spiral, argue a debate round, and land the lead in the school musical without losing a single friend along the way.

He remembered birthdays. Wrote thank-you notes in pen. Took their mom's car to get washed without being asked.

Once, he stayed up late helping Blue finish a science project he barely understood, cutting construction paper with surgeon-like focus, tongue between his teeth.

She hadn't known back then how much quiet a person could carry behind a laugh. But now, when she looked back, she remembered the way the light had looked on the hardwood that evening – soft and slanting, dust motes suspended like breath held too long.

She remembered thinking it smelled like pencil shavings and rosemary chicken.

She remembered not turning around.

Ezra, Blue, and their sister, Aviva, had crammed into the backseat of the car, the last of the relatives waving them out the door. It was normal. Ordinary. Forgettable – until it wasn't.

Dinner was a blur of clinking glasses and crumpled napkins. She remembered leaning against her mother's side, too full, too warm, half-listening to the grown-up conversations about tuition, payments, and apartment leases. She remembered how the sky had looked on the drive home – soft and gold, the first stars faintly blinking awake in the East, the world holding its breath at the edge of night. And she remembered, though she hadn't known to call it fear, the way a strange unease had crept into her ribs. A whisper of wrongness, a ripple in still water.

When they made it home, the house smelled wrong. The porch light was on as she and her family piled into the house with containers of leftovers and a few greeting cards addressed to Ezra.

Inside, the air was heavier. Metallic. The sharpness of it caught at the back of her throat. Her mother called out, once, twice, no answer.

Blue carried on anyway. What else could she do when the world she'd trusted had already split along a fault line she couldn't see yet? There were keys on the counter. A glass tipped over. The soft buzz of the light above the stove, and the smell of something – iron and salt and the terrible finality of it.

And then, a pool across the tile.

A shape slumped where no shape should have been.

The sound her mother made cracked the air wide open. Her father's voice rose sharp and panicked, snapping the silence into two. She stood frozen just inside the doorway, her feet unable to move, her heart hammering against the soft cage of her ribs.

The whole house tilted sideways, and nothing again would be set quite right.

She didn't remember much after that. A local hotel, somehow. The itch of too-bleached bedsheets. The hollow rattle of the air conditioner. Her mother curled herself on the bed, unreachable, sobbing. Her father silent and stone-eyed, staring at the ceiling as if daring God to come down and explain himself.

There were no distractions then. No iPhones nor endless scrolling to pass the hours, just an old metal rack of paperbacks by the vending machines, a lending library. Her eyes settled on a title that felt true against her palm – heavy and cold, *The Stranger*, a stark, unsettling novella that told the tale of Meursault as he grappled with the meaninglessness of life.

She read it once, twice, three times in those endless days.

The words dissolved the moment they touched her- nothing stuck, nothing softened. *The Stranger* was supposed to mean something. She remembered that from class. But Meursault, with his vacant detachment and sun-drenched indifference, felt like an insult.

She wanted to scream at him – to shake him by the shoulders, to beg him to feel something, *anything*. But the book stayed cold in her hands. She kept reading the same line, *I opened myself to the gentle indifference of the world.*

Gentle.

She hated that.

There was nothing gentle about waking up to a world missing her brother.

She clutched the spine hard enough to bend it. Flipped the pages back and forth like it might rewrite itself. But it never did.

The book stayed cold in her hands, just like Rowan's absence. Just like the bedroom door he'd closed behind him.

The funeral happened quickly. Jewish tradition demanded it – dust to dust, without delay.

She remembered the scraping sound of dirt against the casket. The torn black ribbons pinned to their clothes. The mirrors at home were covered with old sheets. The low chairs set out for shiva, where they sat and sat and sat, visitors coming and going like tides. No music. No laughter.

At night, when the mourners left and the house grew too still, she would tiptoe past his bedroom door and pause, just to feel the weight of it. Just to listen to nothing that pressed against her chest.

It wasn't until the seventh day – after the last mourner had gone, after the mirrors were uncovered, after the casseroles spoiled and the house fell too silent again – that she finally opened his door.

The room smelled like him.

Like soap and worn paper, old leather and something warm and human.

It hadn't been sanitized the way the rest of the house had. The air was different – thicker, somehow, like it remembered him. She sat on the floor, back against his bed frame, and let her fingers wander over the shelves, brushing dust that hadn't been wiped away.

And there it was – tucked behind a battered notebook – *The Stranger.*

Dog-eared to ruin. Its cover was soft with handling, the spine cracked so many times it sagged like an over-read prayer book. Underlined passages bled into one another, margins scribbled with half-thoughts and question marks.

He had read it again and again; that much was obvious. She could almost see his hands on the pages, could hear the soft flick of paper and the stillness it wrapped around him. He had folded himself into that book. Into its apathy. Its silence. Its strange, sterile comfort.

And somehow, she'd missed it. The clues were there, waiting in plain sight. And now she could only read them backwards – like a letter sealed after the ink had dried.

Weeks later, when the casseroles turned into trash and the visitors turned into ghosts, a postcard arrived. Three lines:

I'm sorry.
It's nobody's fault.
I just can't stay.

The world cracked open again – quieter this time, but no less devastating. She traced the ink with the tip of her finger, as if she could call him back through the bones of the words.

Years later, under the hush of another early summer evening – Maggie's laughter spinning wild through the air like music – Blue would wonder.

Would Rowan have spun her in the tire swing, strong arms lifting and catching, calling her 'birdie' or 'bug' or some name he made up on the spot, just to make her giggle? Would he have braided flowers into her hair, read her poems with too much drama, taught her how to skip stones across the lake?

She could almost see it – Rowan crouched in the grass beside her, cupping Maggie's tiny hands around a firefly, whispering, "Make a wish, but don't tell."

He would've been the kind of uncle who never forgot a birthday, who showed up late but stayed long, who taught her the chords to "Ripple" before she knew what the lyrics meant.

The kind who carried grief quietly and loved recklessly.

Would he have stood beside her through the years that frayed her? The heartbreaks. The nights she didn't know how to ask for help. The mornings she did. Would he have known what to say – or just known when not to say anything?

She liked to believe so.

And even now, beneath the hush of dusk, with Maggie's joy echoing through the yard and the sky smeared in lilac light, she still did. Somewhere, Rowan was here. Maybe not in form. But in the gentleness he left behind. In the question marks. In the way Maggie laughed with her whole body unafraid.

Some nights she still dreamed of him – not as he was but as he might have been.

Alive.

Laughing.

Building pillow forts with Maggie and her cousins.

Tuning his guitar by firelight.

She lay back in the grass, breathing with the earth beneath her. The blades tickled her arms. Somewhere, a loon called out across the water. Above, the sky was turning. The stars spun out slowly over the lake, each one distant, flickering, barely tethered to her world.

Lives are like rivers, she thought, *In the way they choose their course. Some crash through stone, some carve deep canyons, some slip quietly underground, unseen until they rise again – or don't.*

Rowan's life had been his own to guide. She grieved it still. Loved him fiercely – the boy who once raced her to the dock, who never learned how to say goodbye.

And somewhere beyond the last silver ripples of the lake before her, she believed he knew. Maybe not with words. But with whatever knowing comes after words are gone.

HOW TO SIT WITH THE DYING

The house was quiet when Blue arrived – not the kind of quiet that invited rest, but the kind that settled heavy in the corners, like a sigh no one had let out yet. Lila opened the door in a threadbare sweater, her curls pulled back messily, eyes puffy but dry.

"Thanks for coming," she said, voice low. "She's sleeping. But I think... she knows."

Blue stepped in without needing more. The air inside smelled of old fabric, that specific scent of houses where someone is dying. The kind that clings to the walls, the sheets, to memory. On the kitchen table, a half-drunk mug of tea had gone cold beside a neatly stacked folder labeled with a single word in Lila's looping handwriting: *Estate.*

"She didn't have much," Lila said, as if apologizing. "But I want to make sure what she did have goes where she wanted."

They sat together at the table, Blue opening her laptop slowly, not because the work was difficult, but because the weight of it was real. Death paperwork had a particular ache to it – so much precision for something so ungraspable.

"She's your aunt?" Blue asked softly.

Lila looked away, eyes fixed on a small ivy plant curling around the window frame. "Technically, no. But that's what I call her. She was my mom's ... friend. From back when they both got clean. I don't even know the whole story. My mom's been gone a long time. But Edith – she took me in. Gave me a place to stay when I had nowhere."

She ran her fingers over the rim of the mug, eyes bright but unreadable. "She wasn't easy. But she was steady. You know?"

Blue nodded. She did.

Lila reached for the folder and opened it, revealing yellowed utility bills, a cracked Social Security card, and a will that looked like it had been typed in the '90s. "She used to joke that her final gift to me would be unpaid medical debt and a jar of buttons," Lila said with a weak laugh. "But there's also a ring. Her grandmother's. And I want to make sure it goes to the right person."

Blue skimmed the document. It was simple, but earnest. A few names crossed out, a single line amended in pen, but the sentiment was clear. She wanted Lila to have what little was left.

"Can I ask you something?" Lila asked suddenly.

"Of course."

"How do you sit with all this? With people dying. With grief. Doesn't it ever... get too heavy?"

Blue paused, her fingers still on the keyboard. She thought of Rowan. Of holding his pillow after the wake and trying to memorize the smell. She thought of Maggie's questions about the stars and souls and whether trees missed each other when one was cut down. "It gets heavy," she said. "But not unbearable. Not when you can help someone carry it."

Lila swallowed, eyes filling, "I'm scared, Blue," she whispered. "Not of her dying, exactly. Just – of what's left after. Of what to do with the love that won't have a place to go."

Blue reached across the table and covered her hand. "It still has a place. It just shifts shape."

They sat there like that for a long moment. The computer hummed. The light outside softened into something golden and slow. From the other room, a faint cough stirred the silence, followed by the creak of a bed frame.

"I should check on her," Lila said already standing.

Blue watched her go. Watched the way her body moved like someone learning how to hold two truths at once: hope and goodbye.

She turned back to the documents. There wasn't much to arrange – no accounts to fight over, no properties to divide. Just a life distilled into a few forms and signatures. But Blue moved slowly, handling each paper with care.

When Lila returned, her shoulders were trembling, "She's awake," she said softly, almost not believing it. "She asked if there was music."

Blue stood. "What does she like?"

Lila blinked. "Old soul. Motown. Sam Cooke. She used to sing along while cleaning the kitchen – always off key."

Blue pulled her phone from her coat pocket and opened a playlist she kept for moments like this – soft and full of memory. A voice like smoke and honey filled the room, low and aching.

They stepped into the bedroom together.

Edith lay in a narrow bed by the window, skin waxen and eyes half-lidded but open. Her breaths came shallow but steady. A thin blanket was tucked up to her chin, and the window beside her was cracked just an inch, letting in the scent of leaves and chimney smoke.

She turned her head, "Lila-bird," she rasped.

"I'm here," Lila whispered, taking her hand.

Blue stepped forward, nodding gently. "I'm the lawyer," she said with a soft smile. "We're just making sure your wishes are followed. You've done the hard part."

Edith's lips twitched "About damn time someone cleaned up my mess."

Blue chuckled softly, "You've done more than most."

Lila knelt beside the bed, her hand stroking Edith's with small circular motions. "It's okay if you need to go," she said, voice thick. "You don't have to hold on for me."

Edith blinked slowly. "Not... holding. Just... watching the light." Her eyes flickered toward the window. "It's really nice today."

Blue stepped back then. Not away – just enough to give space. She looked around the room, lined with mismatched furniture, a stack of books on the dresser, and the corner lamp draped in a scarf. A life lived honestly. Not perfect, but full.

"A Change is Gonna Come" began to play.

Edith's lips moved with the chorus, though no sound came.

And then, she was still.

Lila pressed her forehead to Edith's hand. No sobs, not yet. Just presence. Just breath.

Blue moved quietly to the window and opened it wider. The breeze came in like a benediction. The world beyond, unchanged and utterly different.

A crow called from the trees.

The last light of afternoon poured across the bed like grace.

Blue would remember this moment – this room, this air, this stillness. She would remember how love didn't disappear. It just changed form.

Later, Lila would say she didn't know how she got through it. And Blue would tell her, "You stayed. That's how."

HOW TO SIT IN A CIRCLE

The farmhouse sat at the edge of a long gravel drive, framed in goldenrod and the last sunflowers of the season, their heads heavy and bowing toward the earth. The air held that warm, smoky sweetness of early autumn – woodsmoke and ripe apples, something like endings and beginnings tangled up together.

Blue stepped out of her car barefoot, as always, the soles of her feet meeting the dirt like a promise. In the distance, children's laughter spilled from the orchard, high and wild like migrating birds. Somewhere beneath it all, the low, steady hum of women's voices drifted through the wind like music.

A cat leapt down from the porch rail and padded toward her – slender, long-limbed, with thick gray fur like smoke and startling green eyes. She wove around Blue's legs, slow and deliberate, before settling into a patch of sunlight and blinking once as if to say, *You've come back.*

Blue crouched to scratch behind her ears, "Well, hey there," she murmured, "What's your name?"

"Her name's Tova," came a voice from behind.

Blue looked up to see Isla, the owner of the farmhouse, grinning wide as she walked over, arms open for a hug. "She's got a mind of her own, that one. Found her half-frozen in the barn last winter and she hasn't left since."

Blue's chest lifted – not in fear, but in something softer. Tova. A cat with the same name as the midwife who caught Maggie's first breath. That kind of coincidence wasn't something she believed in lightly.

Inside the house, the children played barefoot across the wide pine floors, Maggie among them. There were four in total – Maggie, Isla's daughter, June and niece, Phoebe, and Amy's son, Leo – a tangle of braids and sticky fingers and paint-streaked cheeks.

Isla's kitchen smelled of bread, drying herbs, and some kind of apple spice – a scent so homey it made Blue's shoulders drop the moment she entered.

Outside, yoga mats dotted the grass in a half-circle, each one catching bits of falling leaves. A soft blanket was spread in the middle, its woven edge anchored by smooth stones, with a kettle of tea warming in a wide ceramic bowl.

Rhea—all long limbs and effortless strength—stretched out her arms in a sun pose and welcomed everyone with a low and steady voice. "We'll keep it easy today. Just stretching into breath." Rhea was a certified yoga instructor, though none of the women took this afternoon too seriously.

Blue settled onto a mat near the edge, adjusting the waistband of her leggings and trying not to fuss with the oversized sweatshirt she hadn't quite felt brave enough to peel off. Her body, soft and marked by time, still felt unfamiliar to her in moments like this. But no one here looked like a magazine – hips and bellies were out in full, graceful rebellion.

Beside her, a younger woman rolled out her mat carefully, as if the grass might bite. Her name was Ivy – early twenties, maybe, with unsure hands and a halo of dark curls. She was new to the circle, invited gently by Blue after crossing paths at a library event a few weeks prior. There was something in her – a flicker of hunger and softness that reminded Blue of a much younger version of herself.

"I've never done this before," Ivy whispered, half-laughing. "I think my body is allergic to peace."

Blue smiled, brushing a leaf off her own mat, "That's alright. Mine's still in recovery too."

Rhea invited them to lie down, palms to sky. The hush came gently. "Let your breath soften," Rhea said, "Let it fill the corners of your chest and leave just as slowly. You are held. You are whole. You are not here to be perfect. You are here to return to yourself."

The wind shifted.

"Picture the inside of your body as a warm room," Rhea continued, "A place where nothing is broken. Only becoming."

As Blue breathed deeper, she imagined light pouring through her like tea through muslin. Everything that felt sharp inside her –

the tension behind her eyes, the old grief in her shoulders – began to melt, just a little.

Tova circled behind her head and curled against the edge of her mat, watching with half-lidded eyes. Her purring was steady. A grounding hum.

Afterward, they gathered in a circle with mugs of tea steaming between their palms. Amy passed around a small jar – a salve she'd made with lemon balm and calendula. Isla passed around a loosely packed joint, lit one end with care. Blue took a drag – slow, thoughtful, letting the herb calm what the breath alone could not.

The conversation drifted from birthdays to breakups to brake pads. Abigail was there too, holding space more with her presence than her words. Amy sat cross-legged, her loose braid fraying in the breeze. Rhea laughed easily, her laughter like a warm spill of water over stone.

"I had to call off the engagement," Isla shared quietly. "He didn't want kids. And I just... do."

There was no fixing it.

No rush to respond.

Just nods.

And quiet. And one woman placing her hand softly on another's knee.

Ivy sipped her tea, eyes full and far away. "How do you all make it look so easy?" she asked finally.

Blue shook her head, "It isn't. We're all just patching up the soft spots, over and over." She turned slightly toward Ivy, watching the way the wind brushed her hair back, "You don't need to be strong all the time to be wise. You don't need to be loud to be heard. Sometimes, just showing up is the bravest thing."

Tova – the cat - wove her way through the circle then, rubbing against ankles, tail curling like a question mark. She paused beside Ivy and stared up at her, unblinking. "She likes you," Isla said, matter-of-factly.

Ivy looked down, eyes wide. "I'm ... not really a cat person."

"Doesn't seem to matter," Amy murmured, watching Tova curl around Ivy's crossed legs like she'd found her home.

In the orchard, the kids had begun a leaf fight – flinging gold and amber at each other in gleeful shrieks. Blue watched Maggie chase Phoebe through the rows of trees, their hair streaming behind them like ribbons and laughter trilling like bells in the wind. June piled leaves into a tall mound and leapt in with a scream of joy. Leo inspected the inside of a rotting log with deep concentration.

"Looks like Maggie has a new friend," Amy said, sipping from her mug.

Blue nodded, "That's Phoebe. That is Isla's niece. She's had a rough time lately. Lost her mama this year."

Amy's voice was soft, "Maggie's a good one."

"She is," Blue said, the words sitting warm in her throat.

For a long moment, no one spoke. They just watched the children dance in the orchard light. Leaves fell. The wind shifted. Tova leapt lightly into Isla's lap and began to purr.

Blue closed her eyes, letting the sounds of breath, laughter, and wind fold into her. This was the kind of magic that didn't need explaining – a spell cast in warm cider, in held silence, in the tender ache of being seen and softened by women who understood.

When she opened them again, the light had changed, deepening into amber, slipping slow and low across fields. It was the kind of day you could feel settling into your bones for years.

And Blue, held in the hush of it, whispered inwardly, "Let me remember this. This slowness. This circle. This kindness that spills past the edge of the cup."

Somewhere in the branches above, a bird called out once and was answered.

And the earth, in her oldest voice, breathed back.

HOW TO PLANT A TREE

Maggie burst through the front door, breathless with delight. "Mama!" she called, her cheeks pink with wind, curls springing wildly from her braid. "Look what I got!"

Blue looked up from the sink, hands still wet from rinsing a cutting board. "Whoa," she said, reaching for a towel, "Slow down, baby. What is it?"

Maggie held out a bundle swaddled in damp brown paper and tied with twine. A little tag stuck out, marked in careful third-grade handwriting: *Red Maple*.

"We each got one," Maggie beamed, "From the conservancy field trip, it's for restoration. That means putting something back."

Blue knelt to see it better. A spindly sapling, not much taller than a ruler, its bare roots gently wrapped in moist paper. The beginnings of leaves still curled at the edge like waking hands.

"It's beautiful, Maggie," Blue said softly.

"We get to pick where it goes," Maggie said, already pulling off her shoes. "I want to plant it here, near the creek, so it can drink."

Blue smiled, "Near the creek sounds just right."

They set the sapling on the table while Maggie tugged her damp socks off. Blue turned it gently in her hands, her heart tugged by something unspoken. She could already picture the roots stretching quietly beneath their yard. The shade it would offer – not today, not tomorrow, but someday.

"Want to wait until after dinner?" Blue asked.

Maggie shook her head. "No. Let's do it now before the rain."

Blue glanced at the sky outside the window. Clouds low and blue-gray, the kind that carried thunder in their bellies. She nodded, "Let's do it."

They dressed in jackets and headed out, spade in hand, toward the back of the yard where the grass softened near the water's edge. The creek burbled its song like it always had, patient and tireless.

As they dug, Blue's mind drifted – not away from Maggie, but deeper beneath her. To another tree. One long gone.

It had stood just beyond the edge of her childhood home, an old cottonwood with a trunk wide enough that a group of them could wrap around it, fingers straining to touch. It wasn't technically theirs – it grew on the county side of the property line –

but as a child, Blue hadn't known that. She just knew that it felt like it was theirs. Blue and her siblings and their friends had lived under it. Summer evenings had been shaped by its shade, games of tag and barefoot races around the roots, firefly catching and whispering secrets while leaning against its bark.

When Rowan died, Blue remembered running to that tree, forehead pressed to the rough trunk, and screaming into it until her voice cracked. She remembered how its branches held silence like prayer, and how Ezra later carved a single word into the bark: *Always*.

Years passed, and she had moved away. But she had visited once, during undergrad – driven past the old house on a whim. The tree was still there. Tired, but standing.

And then, years later, it wasn't.

Ezra had called her, bitter. "They widened the road," he'd said. "Cut her down like she was nothing. Said she was a hazard. Said she blocked the line of sight."

Blue didn't cry. Not right away. But when she next visited the spot, now scraped raw and vacant, something inside her ached like bone. She stood where the roots had once been and felt the air miss her. The sky looked too big without that canopy. Too vulnerable.

Even now, she still dreamed of that tree sometimes. In dreams, it was always still standing.

"Is this deep enough?" Maggie asked, tugging Blue gently back to now.

Blue blinked, then nodded. "Yeah, baby. Perfect."

They lowered the sapling into the hole together, fingers covered in cold soil. Maggie cradled the tiny trunk like a newborn.

"Can I say a wish?" Maggie asked.

"You can say anything," Blue assured her.

"I wish it grows strong and happy," Maggie whispered. "I wish it never feels lonely."

Blue touched her daughter's cheek with a muddy hand, "Me too."

Just as they patted the last bit of earth into place, thunder growled low in the distance. Rain began to fall – not in torrents, but a steady soaking drizzle.

Maggie shrieked with laughter, tilting her face to the sky. "It's watering it for us!"

They raced inside, wet and laughing, shedding layers at the door. Maggie disappeared to get dry clothes. Blue stood at the window with a fresh towel in her hands, watching the sapling through the glass.

The rain came down harder, rhythmic and full. She closed her eyes. The sound of it brought her back to Rowan's laugh. To her mother, humming over the dishes while the storm rolled in. That tree – the one they'd lost – it still lived in her body. In every rooted part of her.

She pressed her palm to the cool glass. The creek ran steadily. The sapling stood straight, rain pooling gently at its base.

Behind her, Maggie padded back into the room, warm and dry. She pressed her forehead to Blue's side, "Mama?" she whispered, "Do you think trees remember things?"

Blue smiled, "I think they remember everything."

And as the rain drummed its rhythm on the roof, the new little tree outside drank deeply from the earth, and the old one – the one that was gone – rustled gently in memory.

HOW TO STAND FOR SOMETHING

The night before the protest, Blue and Maggie sat cross-legged on the living room floor, surrounded by paint markers, poster board, and the faint scent of sage from a stick she'd lit earlier. The windows were open to the late spring breeze, and the dusk outside held a tangerine glow, warm and moody. Maggie dipped her brush into purple paint, tongue poked out in focus.

"Can I come with you tomorrow?" she asked, not looking up from her poster-in-progress, which read in slanted block letters: *Kindness is a Revolution.*

Blue looked over, heart tugging. "I think you can," she said slowly. "If we stay together and it's peaceful. You're part of this, too. This world we're trying to protect."

Maggie beamed. "I'll bring Mr. Bunz. He's good at standing up for things." They laughed. Blue leaned forward and painted a sunflower on her own sign, then another. Beneath them, she wrote: *No Earth. No Us.*

They talked as they painted – about fairness, about love being love, about the importance of teachers and doctors and music and libraries. About how some leaders don't lead, they silence. Maggie asked why people would ever want to take things away from others.

Blue didn't have a clear answer.

When they finished, they lined the signs along the hallway to dry. Maggie's were bright and a little wobbly. Blue's were bold and fierce. Then Blue pulled out her guitar and they curled up on the couch, Maggie leaning into her side, her hair still smelling faintly of lavender from the bath.

Blue brushed a hand through her daughter's curls and softly sang a tune she'd made up when Maggie was just a baby.

> *You are made of river light,*
> *Roots that hold through darkest night.*
> *Little star, keep burning true,*
> *The world is better all because of you.*

Maggie yawned, content. "I like that one, Mama."

The morning of the protest dawned warm and restless. They dressed in layers – Blue in a worn denim jacket with patches and buttons, Maggie in a rainbow hoodie and mismatched socks. They tucked fruit and granola bars into a canvas tote and grabbed their signs.

The park was already humming by the time they arrived. The protest had grown out of weeks of bruising policy cuts to healthcare, restrictions on reproductive rights, funding gutted for schools and the arts.

Whispers of legislation aimed at queer families and non-traditional parenting had reached even their small town.

It wasn't just politics anymore – it was personal.

For Blue.

For Eli.

For every single person standing in the dewy grass with signs raised and coffee cooling in compostable cups.

A banner fluttered between two birch trees: *We Rise Together*

And, they did.

Blue adjusted the strap of her bag on her shoulder and took Maggie's hand, "Stay close, okay?"

"I'm ready," Maggie nodded seriously, holding her sign like a sword.

The crowd was beautiful in its chaos: queer couples with babies in slings, grandmothers handing out buttons, teenagers weaving through the crowd with wild eyes and handmade shirts. Blue spotted Abigail and Isla near a patch of sun-drenched lawn where volunteers passed out buttons, flyers, and bottles of water. She smiled at Abigail's shirt, which read: *Make Art, Not Empire*.

And then suddenly, Eli was there – just like they'd planned.

Their kind of date: no wine, no candlelight. Just pavement and purpose, shared breath and bright signs. Her heart jumped anyway, the way it always did when she spotted him across a crowd. Especially when she saw who was with him – Shilo on one side, Sade on the other, their protest signs loud with glitter and conviction.

He gave her a look that said, "We showed up. We're here."

And she smiled like it was more than enough.

Blue blinked in surprise, then smiled widely, "I didn't know you were coming."

"I didn't know you were bringing Maggie," he said, a small smile curving his lips. "Guess great minds think alike."

Sade hugged Maggie immediately. Shilo gave a cool nod and leaned his sign against a bench: *Justice is Grown, Not Given*.

Blue reached out, touching Eli's elbow – grounding herself in the one familiar anchor in the swirl.

He turned, and there was that breath between them.

That hush before a truth.

She leaned in and kissed him – not a grand kiss, but a steady one. Like the clasp of fingers before stepping into a current.

He smiled into it, like he already knew the water would be cold, but worth it.

The speeches began, then chants. A woman in a wheelchair led a call-and-response. An elder held a drum, tapping out a heartbeat rhythm. Nearby, someone had brought a guitar – an older woman in a faded flannel and a big straw hat. She stood under the birch trees, strumming softly at first, then louder as a small group gathered. Blue smiled, grateful for the sound and its spirit, but stayed where she was. It wasn't about being seen – it was about standing together, quiet and rooted, part of something larger than herself.

Eli stood behind her, his hand resting lightly on the small of her back – steady, grounding, a silent rhythm in her spine.

Shilo clapped along, eyes bright beneath a hand-drawn ball cap, the kind kids wore when they'd made their own rules.

Sade danced with Maggie, their protest signs tossed gently to the grass, spinning like maple seeds caught in joy – wild, weightless, unafraid.

Blue's voice caught only once, and it was when she saw a little boy standing on an overturned milk crate, holding a sign twice his size that read: *My Mom Deserves Healthcare*.

The crowd grew, and with it, so did something electric – not rage, but resolve.

Not chaos, but courage.

When the march began, Eli reached for her hand, fingers calloused, familiar. Maggie grabbed Sade's with the same quiet conviction, and the five of them moved into the street as one.

Not a couple. Not a family.

Something bigger.

A constellation.

Surrounded by strangers who felt like kin.

There was rhythm to their feet, to their breath, to the echo of chants bouncing off the buildings like birdsong.

They walked for love. For the future. For teachers and scientists, and artists. For forests and clean water. And in the still moments between shouts, when the wind stirred the trees just right, Blue swore she could hear the earth humming beneath them: *Keep going, it said. You're not alone. You were made for this.*

HOW TO GET A JOB

The sun leaned low against the windows of Ellis McCrae's office, casting long, honey-colored slats across the polished wood of the conference table. Blue sat at its edge with a legal pad open, her pen stilled mid-sentence. Outside, the breeze stirred in the last of the oak leaves, their fluttering shadows dancing across the floor like they were whispering something just out of reach.

She was used to this kind of quiet – the good kind. The kind that came from being around someone who didn't need to prove anything. Ellis was across from her, half-lost in a dense paragraph about charitable disbursements and mineral rights, his glasses slipping down the bridge of his nose in that familiar, meticulous way. His suit was tailored, but not fussy. A man who'd been dressing like this since the kind of meetings where he was the youngest one in the room.

They were reviewing a high-profile estate file – an old Michigan family with generations of timber money and a labyrinth of trusts that twisted around lakefront properties and grandfather clocks. Blue knew these kinds of cases well enough by now, but something about this one had a heavier feel. Not because of its value, but its weight. The client's name – Graham Dean – sat on the file tab in sharp black ink. She didn't react, not outwardly. But something inside shifted.

Ellis cleared his throat lightly and circled a line near the bottom of the page. "We'll need clarity on the granddaughter's clause. If the other heirs contest, sentiment won't carry the day."

Blue nodded, eyes scanning the document without really reading. "We can expand the statement of intent. Her letters are archived – we could include excerpts."

He made a soft sound of agreement. Then he leaned back slightly, spine pressing into the leather of his chair. The sunlight brushed his jawline, catching the silver at his temples and the dust floating lazily between them.

The sunlight caught on the edge of a photo frame near the corner of Ellis's desk, and Blue's eyes landed there, not because she didn't know what it held, but because she did. Miles McCrae, grinning in a cap and gown, stood beside his parents on the courthouse steps. Blue had seen the photo a hundred times – on his desk, in Christmas cards, in stories told in that understood way Ellis did, like pride wasn't something to be broadcast, just quietly held.

Today, though, the image caught her differently. Not because of the smile, or the degree, or even the uncanny resemblance between father and son – but because of the light. The way it lit the edge of the frame, the reflection of the glass. The way time folded in on itself without warning.

She remembered when that photo was taken. Miles had passed the bar the same summer Blue finally felt steady again. She remembered the small celebration at the office, the cake someone brought from the co-op bakery, Ellis's rare half-crooked smile when he said, "It's strange watching your kid walk into the same storm you've just come out of."

Maybe it was the light in the room, or the wind in the trees, or the way the name on the folder in front of them still echoed in her chest. But suddenly she was back there, before any of this. Before she had a title, or a reputation, or even much faith in her own feet.

Back when she still flinched at the sound of tires on gravel.

Back when she bled and went anyway.

It had been morning – a Thursday. Maggie was eight months old and chewing on a silicone giraffe at the edge of the kitchen. Blue had been ready for over an hour – hair pinned, blouse tucked, resume printed three times just in case. The coffee she poured sat untouched on the counter. She kept glancing at the clock. She told herself it was fine. Silver Hollow was small. The law office was only ten minutes away. But still, she waited. The interview was at 9:30. She had planned to leave by 9:00. It was 8:48.

Dean hadn't answered her text.

She repacked the diaper bag, her movements careful and rehearsed. Bottles, pacifier, backup clothes. Maggie blew spit bubbles, unconcerned. Blue touched her hair again, checking for static. She adjusted her collar. The bruise on her collarbone wasn't there yet. Not yet.

Dean's car pulled in with a crunch of gravel, music leaking from the windows. She opened the door before he knocked. He didn't greet her. Just lifted his sunglasses and said, "Running late. Traffic on 31."

She didn't reply. Just reached for the baby bag and turned toward the kitchen. As she handed him the bottles, she murmured, "You were supposed to be here thirty minutes ago."

He bristled instantly. "You always do this."

"Do what?" she asked, still calm, still not meeting his eyes.

"Act like you're the only one with somewhere to be. You think I don't have shit going on?"

She held his gaze now, tired. "Dean, I have a job interview. That's it. I just need you to be on time."

He stepped forward – not close enough to crowd her, but close enough that his voice dropped. "You know what, Blue? You're always counting the minutes. You want everything perfect."

"I just don't want to lose this opportunity," she said quietly, adjusting Maggie's jacket as the baby squirmed in his arms.

And then, so fast she didn't register it until it landed – he lashed out. Not a punch, not even a shove. Just the heel of his hand caught her chest, knocking her slightly off balance. She stumbled back to the edge of the counter, breathing hard. The strap of her bag dug into the spot just above her collarbone. That would be the part that bloomed blue.

Dean froze. His face paled, his mouth opened. "Shit. Blue. I didn't – I didn't mean – "

She didn't want to hear the rest. She straightened, adjusted her blouse, and reached for her coat. She didn't cry. She didn't yell. She just handed him the baby bag with a voice like smoke.

"She napped. Bottles are labeled. I'll be back by four."

He stood there, dumb with apology. But the door was already closing behind her.

The air outside had felt too clean. The wind sharp, full of song, and cold sun. Her car seat was warm from the sun, and the radio came on mid-chorus. She didn't remember the drive. Just the door with his name on it: *Ellis McCrae, Estate & Legacy Law*.

He met her in the lobby himself. No assistant, no handshake. Just a nod and a glance toward his office, "Ms. Katz?"

She nodded, smoothing her skirt with her palm.

They talked for forty-five minutes. About the structure of trusts, sure. About probate timelines. But also about community.

About grief. About what it meant to help someone put their love into writing before they were gone. He asked what drew her to this kind of work.

She hadn't meant to say anything personal, but her voice came out low and certain. "Because the first time I really understood the law was when I was trying to protect what little I had left."

Ellis studied her for a long moment. Then he offered her the job with only a few words, "If you want it, it's yours."

Blue blinked, the light from the window glancing off the brass photo frame again. She could still feel the weight of the past pressed quietly against the edge of her ribs, but not like before. Not like a wound. More like a scar that knew its shape and no longer ached when she breathed deep.

Ellis slid the file toward her. "You'll finish the Dean draft?"

She nodded, "Of course."

He paused, "You know, I was proud of you before I knew why."

Blue met his eyes. Not surprised. Just still. "Thank you," she said softly, and turned toward the window. The leaves were beginning to fall, slow and golden. Somehow, they always trusted the ground to catch them.

HOW TO SHINE ON

The festival map had been passed around like an heirloom, its edges soft with fingerprints and beer-ringed corners. Hand-drawn pine trees curled along the borders, little stars marking the music tents and the fire circles and the vendors who sold tinctures in sun-dyed glass bottles. Blue folded it into her pocket without really needing it. This kind of place – wild, warm, humming with barefoot people and djembe drums – was stitched into her bones.

They had arrived just before sunset, the four of them: Blue and Connor, Abigail and Charlie.

The gravel lot crackled underfoot as they stepped out, dust rising like breath around their ankles. Blue took a long inhale – pine, bonfire, the sharp tang of something herbal – and felt the tension unspool from her shoulders.

Connor hoisted the cooler onto his shoulder without being asked, his free hand resting briefly on Blue's lower back as they started down the trail. Abigail laced her fingers through Charlie's and pointed out the handmade signs staked between tree trunks

– *Reiki / Medic Tent / Free Hugs*. Charlie laughed softly, amused and maybe a little skeptical, his boots crunching behind her.

The forest trail was lit by strings of solar lanterns, casting soft halos onto the mossy path. Laughter floated like pollen on the air, and the sound of a mandolin rose up from somewhere near the clearing.

A child with fairy wings darted past, fireflies in full pursuit. Someone had hung a sign from a crooked cedar - driftwood and paint smudged with years of weather and welcome: *Welcome to Wildlight*.

Connor tipped his head toward it and said, "Think they'll still let us in if we forgot our flower crowns?"

Blue smiled, "Speak for yourself."

She pulled a crumpled band of wildflowers from her bag, pressed flat between her journal pages, and tucked it into her hair with quiet ceremony.

Abigail spun once in the dappled light, arms wide, already humming to the rhythm of some distant drumbeat.

Charlie just shook his head, but not unkindly – the kind of look you give someone you'd follow anywhere.

The sign was still there – a mosaic with broken glass, sea glass, and bottle shards pieced together into a shimmer of color and memory. *Welcome to Wildlight*, it read, the letters sun-faded but still glowing with something ancient. Blue had first danced beneath it as a teenager, bare feet stomping into the packed earth, cider sloshing from a paper cup. Later, she'd carried Maggie through it in a soft sling, humming along with a fiddle tune, pointing out the fairy lights and dreamcatchers strung between trees.

Now she stepped beneath it – the painted sign swaying gently overhead – with Connor at her side, his hand warm and steady at the small of her back.

The air smelled like smoke and sage, and somewhere deeper in the woods, a drumbeat pulsed low and slow, like a heartbeat underground.

She didn't feel old.

She felt weathered in the good way – like driftwood, like something softened by time and made more beautiful by the wear.

"You've got that smile," Connor murmured, leaning down slightly so only she could hear. "The one that says this place is sacred."

Blue laughed softly, the sound more breath than voice. "It kind of is," she said, eyes scanning the path ahead – the lanterns swaying, the firelight flickering through branches, the hum of belonging rising like mist.

Connor didn't say anything more. He just stayed close, hand still at her back, like a promise.

The festival opened up like a field of stars. Vendors offered patchouli soaps and fiber art. The food trucks served coconut rice bowls and fermented sodas, heirloom tomato sandwiches, and mushroom tacos with lime crema. They ate sitting cross-legged in the grass, knees brushing, Abigail wide-eyed at the whole scene, and Charlie already barefoot, his arm comfortably around Abigail as they swayed slightly to the rhythm of a nearby guitar.

By nightfall, the stage lit up under a canopy of prayer flags, and the music deepened into something that moved through bodies like a tide. Blue danced with Connor under strings of lanterns, her skirt twirling, hair loose and wild. She spun with strangers and laughed with her head thrown back, the drums pulsing in her chest. Around her, joy bloomed in every direction—unruly, radiant, impossible to hold.

And she let it grow.

Later that night, after the last brass-fueled jam crescendoed and the lanterns dimmed low, they followed a whispering path toward the lake. Charlie led the way with a glow stick tucked into his bandana, and Abigail, tipsy and barefoot, giggled quietly as she navigated roots and moonlight, holding his hand. The trail opened to the water like a held breath, soft sand and the hush of midnight ripples folding into the shore.

Blue slipped out of her dress without speaking, it felt natural, like shedding skin, like a rite. Abigail hesitated for a heartbeat, then followed with a breathless laugh, "I can't believe I'm doing this," she whispered.

Charlie whooped and ran in first, kicking up waves and laughter, splashing and moonlight into wild arcs that scattered across the surface like silver sparks. Abigail called after him, shaking her head but smiling, one hand still tangled in her skirt hem.

Connor stood at the edge, watching as Blue undressed – not with hunger, but with something gentler. Reverence, yes. But also, memory.

Like he was watching a woman step into herself, not away from anything, but toward something whole. She slid off her dress slowly, bare feet pressing into the soft lake bed silt.

Connor peeled off his shirt, quiet and certain, and followed her into the shadows.

The water caught her like an old friend.

Cool, wrapping around her thighs, pulling a breath from her lips.

The moon spilled across her shoulders.

Behind her, Connor's hand found hers beneath the surface – no words, just the warm shock of contact, and the lake holding them both.

The lake was cold at first, and then perfect. The kind of cold that made you laugh with your whole body. Blue floated on her back, arms spread wide, hair fanning behind her. The moon was nearly full, caught between branches and reflections.

Connor swam to her side, not touching her at first, just close enough that she could feel the warmth of him beneath the surface – a pulse in the water, steady and quiet.

She turned slightly, just enough to catch his eyes in the moonlight. There was no teasing in them. Just awe.

"You've got silver in your hair," he said, his voice low, almost reverent. "It catches in the light, like river threads."

She stilled at that—not because it embarrassed her, but because it didn't. Because it felt like something she'd been waiting a long time to hear.

The silence between them deepened, but didn't grow heavy. The lake held it gently, like it held them.

She turned her head. "That's new."

"I like it," he said. "It suits you. Like a story that's been told well."

She ducked beneath the water and surfaced closer, arms around his neck. "You always say the right thing," she whispered.

"No," he assured, "Just the true thing."

Behind them, Abigail and Charlie splashed like kids, howling at the stars. Blue tilted her head to the sky. The whole world felt suspended, like a song held on its last chord.

She kissed Connor there, under the moon and the soft drumming of distant fire circles, with the water holding them up like memory.

Her arms around his shoulders, his hands steady at her waist, they moved together in a rhythm older than words. The years slipped off her like clothing – not shed in shame, but in release.

For the first time in a long time, she let herself feel completely beautiful, not despite the years, but because of them.

Because of what she had survived. Because of what her body still remembered how to feel. And the lake, and the firelight, and the moon – they all seemed to agree.

In the morning, Blue woke before the others. She slipped out barefoot, wrapped in a sweater, and wandered toward the lake. Coffee simmered in a dented enamel pot by the fire circle. Someone with gray hair and a banjo strummed a tune she didn't know but remembered anyway.

She sat on a mossy rock, mug cradled in her hands, and watched the sun rise pink and gold through the trees. And for once, she didn't need to chase the moment or make sense of it.

It was enough to feel it.

HOW TO LISTEN WHEN IT'S QUIET

The house was quiet in a way that felt unnatural, like the silence that settles in just before a branch breaks. Maggie had left with Dean just after dinner, her backpack slung over one shoulder, curls still damp from the bath. Blue had kissed her forehead, said, "Have fun, be safe," and smiled for her daughter's sake — but inside, a small, familiar ache had already begun to bloom.

There was no message to say they'd arrived. Dean never sent one. He wasn't the type to reassure. He moved through the world assuming nothing would go wrong, and if it did, it would somehow be someone else's fault. Blue knew better. She had lived long enough to know that safety was not a guarantee, not even for the innocent.

She walked through the house slowly, switching off lights as if dimming the world would soften the absence. Without Maggie, the rooms felt shadowed, as though the very air missed her. Her daughter was the pulse of the house — warm and bright and always in motion. Without her, the corners stretched darker. Her voice, her laughter, the trail of books and markers she left behind

— gone in an instant. What remained was stillness. Not quite peace. Not quite grief. Just that suspended breath between what is and what was.

Blue lit a candle in the kitchen, not because she needed the light, but because she needed the flame. She watched it flicker and dance, the scent of beeswax rising, subtle and familiar. She touched a finger to the melted edge, letting the warmth anchor her.

She leaned into the light like it might speak.

The quiet was different tonight. It came on slowly, like mist, settling into her bones. There was no hum from Maggie's tablet. No gentle rustling of blankets or creak of footsteps above. Blue felt it in her chest, that old pull—memory blooming in the body before the mind could catch up.

She moved to the living room and crouched beside the fireplace. The kindling basket was nearly empty, but she found a few good pieces: splinters from a broken chair leg, a pine branch stripped of needles, and a small bundle of paper she didn't bother to unfold. She fed the fire carefully, one offering at a time. The ritual of it soothed her. Hands busy. Mind loose. The fire gave shape to something shapeless. She didn't name the feeling. She just let it rise.

And then, as the flames began to take, it came back—not all at once, but in pieces. The dark days of the storm. Cold seeping in under the doors. The silence wasn't quiet, not really, but something deeper. She and so many others had shivered in that long pause, unplugged from the world. There had been no hum of distant streetlights, no static from a forgotten TV, no buzz of incoming calls — just candles and the low groan of the wind moving through the trees like a warning.

It wasn't loneliness she'd felt back then. It was something else. Something elemental. A kind of stillness that pressed in on all sides, like the world was caught in a breath between endings and beginnings. She remembered staring into the darkness then, and feeling not fear, but recognition. As if the world, stripped bare, looked a little more like her.

Blue didn't name it now. She didn't need to. Her body remembered.

She let her shoulders drop. Let her jaw unclench. A small mercy. One she gave herself.

She stood slowly, the joints in her knees crackling like twigs, and crossed to the bookshelf. Nestled between dry legal texts, the cedar box felt like a secret. The wood had darkened with age, but still gave off that faint, resinous scent – sharp and sweet, like forest altars and campfires long burned out. Inside was her tarot deck.

The cards smelled faintly of cedar and rose, the scent of old stories and something older still. The woman who'd given them to her — a professor's wife she'd met during undergrad — had pressed the deck into her hands like a secret. Blue still remembered her voice, "For when logic fails you, she'd said, and you need to feel your way forward instead."

She had used them rarely in recent years, tucked them away when law school demanded facts, not feelings. But tonight, with Maggie gone and the house echoing with silence, she craved something less structured. Something that could speak in symbols and silences.

She shuffled carefully, the cards whispering against each other like dry leaves. Then she drew three and laid them gently on the table. The room breathed with her. The fire behind her popping as if to say, *I'm here. I'm here.*

The first: *The Moon*. A silver path winding between twin towers. A dog and a wolf bristling at the water's edge, unsure what to trust. In the sky above, the moon gazed down – full and knowing, but half-veiled in mist. The light wasn't clear. It shimmered in a way that made Blue's breath catch, like it was about to show her something and then didn't.

She thought of the feeling just before a memory returns – that shimmer of knowing, just beyond reach. The way intuition can hum louder than fact.

The second: *The Six of Cups*. Two children in a garden, the taller offering a cup filled with white flowers to the smaller. A gesture so tender it almost hurt to look at. The buildings in the background blurred into watercolor grays, as if the world beyond the moment no longer mattered. The smaller child's feet were just slightly lifted, like she might run – or stay forever.

Blue's chest ached with recognition. That was Maggie. That was her. The part of her that still wanted to believe in safe gardens, in slow kindness, in things that could last.

The third: *The Queen of Pentacles.* A woman seated on a carved stone throne, one hand resting over a heavy gold coin in her lap. Ivy curled around her feet, and a rabbit peeked from the corner of the card – soft, alert. Her gaze wasn't regal, but kind. Watchful. There were fur-lined robes, but her bare foot touched the earth. A crown but no pretense.

This was who she wanted to be. Grounded. Tender. Certain. A woman who could keep her eyes soft even when the world turned sharp.

Blue let out a breath she hadn't realized she was holding. The fire crackled behind her, and the candle's flame had burned low, forming a soft golden ring around the wick. Outside, the wind picked up. Somewhere in the distance, a single branch fell.

She leaned back, her hands resting on her thighs, and closed her eyes. The cards weren't answers. They never had been. But they were something else — reminders, maybe. That she wasn't lost.

That even now, the earth was still holding her.

That there was meaning in staying present.

That this quiet was not emptiness, but invitation.

And she was listening.

HOW TO LOVE

The woods had thinned with the season. Bare branches reached like ribs toward a pale October sky, and beneath them, Blue moved slowly, deliberately, boots pressing into damp earth. Birchbend Loop was familiar, a trail she had walked in all moods, all weathers. Today, it was quiet enough to hear her breath and the papery rustle of a squirrel somewhere up ahead. She welcomed the stillness.

Connor had left that morning before the sun, kissing her forehead and murmuring something about catching a run before work. His mouth had been soft. But his eyes – not cold, just distant. She knew the shape of silence when it sat between two people.

It had started the night before, over lentil stew and sourdough. They were washing dishes together when Connor's phone buzzed on the counter. He picked it up without hesitation, thumbed it open, and turned the screen toward her.

"Isn't it a great picture?" he said with a small grin.

It was a selfie – Connor, laughing in the golden light of a park trail, cheek pressed to Camille's. Blue knew her name. She had met her at a bonfire over the summer. Camille had kind eyes and a quiet warmth, the kind of woman who could coax a room into laughter with nothing but a glance. In the photo, her hand rested lightly on Connor's shoulder, not possessive – just comfortable, like someone who had been let in and had chosen to stay.

Blue smiled automatically and sincerely. It was a great picture. They looked easy together. Happy.

But later, as she folded Maggie's laundry and tucked the smaller socks into pairs, the image floated back to her – not sharp with jealousy but softened with awareness. The tug of longing. The ache of feeling momentarily peripheral to someone she loved deeply. Not forgotten. Just... not held in that moment. Like the light had shifted ever so slightly, and she wasn't sure if she'd stepped into shadow, or if it had always been there.

And that, strangely, was what brought Ezra to mind. Not because she was angry, but because this ache – this subtle loneliness that arrived even in love – reminded her how complex closeness could be.

Her older brother, Ezra, had always worn arrogance like cologne – too thick, a bit nauseating, but not entirely disingenuous. He was a man who dressed head-to-toe in fan gear, proudly quoting scores and player stats he barely understood, nodding solemnly at sports headlines while sipping his overpriced craft beer. There was something performative in everything he did, even his casual lean against a kitchen counter. And yet, Blue loved him. He was still her brother. Still the boy who once helped her to climb the barn rafters to watch summer storms roll in.

Years ago, when things had begun to unravel between Ezra and his wife, Blue had gone over to talk. His wife had called her in tears, a voice trembling with a sadness too familiar. Blue had arrived to find Ezra in the garage, leaning back in a lawn chair, cracking jokes about their fantasy football league while rearranging a shelf of screwdrivers for the third time.

"She's being dramatic," he said between sips. "It wasn't even that serious. It was just a few messages. Maybe a drink."

Blue had leaned against the doorframe, arms crossed. "So, it happened?"

Ezra didn't answer right away. Instead, he launched into small talk, as if the tension in the air didn't smell like guilt. He asked about Maggie, made a half-hearted joke about Blue being a heartbreaker. Then finally, as though offering a gift, he said, "It's not like you would understand. You never even settled down."

Blue had stood there, hands tucked into her sleeves, feeling something in her heart go quiet. She didn't argue. But she did meet his eyes and say gently, "There's more than one way to love fully."

She just remembered.

Remembered how, when someone loves you from fear, it comes out as control. How, when you are only half-trusted, you become half-seen. And how Ezra had mistaken secrecy for freedom, and shame for intimacy.

His wife, a woman whose name Blue barely heard anymore because Ezra rarely said it, had once been kind to Blue. Quiet, refined, with an understated beauty – she wore pain like pearls, strung carefully behind tight smiles. Blue had always suspected she knew more than she let on, and it broke her heart to think of the loneliness she must have endured in Ezra's shadow.

The wind lifted a lock of Blue's hair, and she tucked it behind her ear. She thought of Connor now. Of how he hadn't hidden the photo. He shared it openly. Of how hard it must have been to speak the words aloud. And how grateful she was that he had.

She pulled a water bottle from her coat pocket – covered in peeling stickers from record stores, climate marches, indie bookstores, and music festivals. The metal clinked softly against the stone as she set it beside her. She stared at the water, the way it moved without rushing.

Then, as if remembering something urgent and sacred, Blue pulled her phone from her bag and texted Connor:

> *Hey. About that picture of you and Camille. You looked happy. I'm glad you shared it with me. I noticed something in myself last night – that quiet tug of feeling a little outside the frame. Not jealousy, just ... old patterns. But I see you. I see how openly*

you love. And I'm grateful. You're not an afterthought. You are a part of my center.

She hesitated, then added, *You're kind of magic.*

The words glowed on the screen a moment before she hit send. She imagined his face when he read it – maybe a small shake of the head, maybe a smile he wouldn't show just anyone.

Only then did she pull her journal from her bag, fingers red from the wind, and write without lines: *Love is not always easy. Sometimes it is the bravery of being seen and staying anyway.*

And in her chest, a quiet blooming: not joy, exactly. But something like peace.

Something better.

HOW TO LEAVE

The morning was slow and gold – the kind of morning she'd have bottled if she could.

Maggie was in a whirl of untamed curls and laughter, spinning slow pirouettes across the dew-wet grass as they made their way to the car. She clutched a hand-drawn card in one hand – a lopsided heart scrawled in crayon – her end-of-the-year gift for her favorite teacher.

Blue watched her, feeling her chest ache the way it sometimes did when life felt too beautiful to be safe. She bent down, tucking a loose curl behind Maggie's ear, pressing a kiss on her forehead that smelled of honey shampoo and wild air.

"Be kind today," Blue whispered, "Be you."

Maggie beamed, the missing front tooth in her smile making her look more wildflower than child. "I will, Mama!" she called, bounding through the school doors without looking back.

Blue stood there a moment longer than necessary, letting the warmth of the sun, the earth, and her own quiet gratitude wrap around her like a shawl. The earth itself seemed to hum under her feet.

At work, the hours unfolded unmiraculously, but with gentle purpose. She greeted her coworkers with a nod and an easy smile, sliding into her modest corner of the small firm. No sharp suits or leather chairs here – just battered desks, worn coffee mugs, a window cracked open to let in the green breath of summer, and any song shared by the birds who flew by.

She spent the morning helping an elderly woman sort out a messy stack of estate papers. She could have been impatient, could have waved her through with a quick signature and a half-hearted explanation. Instead, she pulled up a chair, smoothed the papers out one by one, and listened.

The woman's eyes were clouded with age but still fierce, softened by the end. "You explain things better than any lawyer I've ever met," she'd said, patting Blue's hand with surprising strength.

Blue just smiled. No need to correct her. Kindness didn't ask for applause. When the meeting with her client had finished, she returned to her desk, where someone had left wildflowers in a chipped coffee cup waiting for her. No note, no name, just a small, breathing gift.

She didn't need to know who had left them. Beauty, she believed, didn't owe you explanations.

She worked steadily through the afternoon, drafting wills, clarifying documents, answering questions with the patience of someone who still believed people deserved to be understood. There was a low-grade buzz of contentment under it all – a life not perfect but chosen.

That evening, she had plans.

A picnic with Connor.

She pictured it easily: the kind of soft evening they had come to fall into without effort – coolers packed, a guitar slung in the trunk, a quilt spread wide across the tall grass by the lake.

She could already see it: Maggie's laughter echoing earlier that afternoon like birdsong. The hush of twilight setting low. The scent of basil and lake air, the soft fizz of cider cans, the hum of a melody half-remembered.

Connor's hand pressed lightly against hers – not a grip, just contact. Just presence. And just beyond the quilt, a cluster of milkweed swayed in the breeze, their pods beginning to split.

One tuft lifted – fragile, silvered – catching the light as it rose and drifted upward, directionless and sure.

She'd watch it go, breath caught in her chest, and think how beautiful it was – not knowing where you'd land, only that you'd been carried.

– HOW TO LEAVE

She didn't know this was the last evening. Only that it was full, and golden, and enough.

There was still so much to do – dinner to pack, Maggie's schoolwork to sign, phone calls to return – but none of it felt heavy. It felt like living. She tapped a text into her phone, smiling without meaning to.

> *You bring strawberries; I'll bring the music.*

The response came almost immediately – a string of hearts and a promise of cold drinks and bad jokes.

The windows of the car were down when she pulled away from the office parking lot. The air smelled like lilacs and cut grass, and warm asphalt. A song she didn't recognize floated up from the radio – a slow, rolling guitar and a raspy, low voice. She hummed along anyway.

The sun was dropping lazy gold across the road ahead. The lake beyond it shimmered, breathing and inviting. She leaned into the curve of the road, the hum of tires on pavement, the thrum of her own heart beating steady and soft.

The world felt wide open, forgiving, and holy. And then –

A sound.

A flash.

A swerve.

A rupture.

A silence so big it swallowed the world whole.

The wildflowers on the passenger seat tumbled forward, petals scattering across the dashboard. The song on the radio cut out mid-note. The sunlight fractured into shards on the broken glass. Her name echoed somewhere – distant, tender, desperate.

And then, even that was gone.

HOW TO STAY

The house was quiet.

Not the quiet of sleeping children or a storm waiting to break, but the kind that settles after something has already been taken. That heavy stillness that seeps into floorboards and cups, that presses itself into the linen curtains and the seams of worn couches, waiting to be named.

Maggie had stopped asking. She just moved like someone who knew that the world was different now, even if no one had said so out loud. She stayed barefoot all morning, trailing bits of creek mud across the wood floors, her face tilted toward the window like she was listening for something the rest of them couldn't hear. When Connor offered her breakfast, she nodded without looking, her hand resting on the spine of a book she wasn't reading.

In the bathroom, the mirror above the sink had been covered with a square of soft muslin. Someone had done it without fuss. A gesture that said, *We will not look for ourselves in this loss. Not yet.*

There was a single yahrzeit candle on the windowsill. It had burned through most of the night. Caleb had found it in a drawer, still in its box. He hadn't asked. Just lit it and left it burning. Now the wax pooled low and pale, as if even the flame was mourning slowly.

Outside, the soil thawed. Ezra stood with a shovel in the garden, not digging, not planting – just standing there like a man who couldn't remember what he was doing. His boots were clean. His mouth was pressed into a line. Maggie passed him once, on her way to the creek, and he didn't move. She didn't stop.

The sound of a car engine idling pulsed faintly at the edge of the woods. Dean.

He hadn't come inside. He stood beside his SUV, phone in one hand, the other resting uselessly on the roof rack. Miriam, Blue's mother, had glanced through the window and said nothing. Her father, David, hadn't looked up at all.

It was unclear if he'd been invited or if he'd just driven up to let Maggie come and go as she needed. Either way, no one crossed the gravel drive to greet him.

Ezra finally walked to the driveway. Not quickly, like someone being pulled there. He stood beside the hood of the car and said, "You shouldn't be here."

Dean didn't respond at first. His eyes were rimmed with red, but dry. "You think I don't know that?" he said eventually. "You think I haven't lived every day knowing what I did to her?"

Ezra's face hardened.

Dean nodded once. "She still held me while I cried the night my mom passed. She still covered for me when I missed Maggie's preschool performance. She was better to me than I deserved."

Ezra opened his mouth – then shut it again.

The fight drained out of his arms. He turned without another word. Dean didn't follow. He just leaned against the car and stared into the woods.

Inside, Lila sat cross-legged on the floor, eyeliner smudged, picking at the threads of a rug Blue once brought from a local artist because it "felt like walking on moss." Lila hadn't spoken in hours.

Abigail sat beside her, one arm loosely around her shoulders, humming an old folk tune under her breath – something about rivers leaving and the sky. Neither of them cried. Not in that moment. Just breath in unison.

Amy was in the kitchen, sleeves rolled up, barefoot, hair pinned back loosely. Leo stood beside her on a stool, small fingers stirring slow circles in the pot with solemn concentration. The soup wasn't for healing. It was for anchoring. The kitchen needed a sound, and this was what they knew how to make. Amy moved without speaking, just nodding when Leo reached for more thyme, touching his back when he leaned too far over the pot.

Tova arrived midday. No announcement. Just the hush that followed her in. She carried a sprig of rosemary, and a bundle of cedar wrapped in soft black cloth. She lit nothing. She said very little. She placed the herbs gently near the candle and ran her hands along the windowsill as if checking for heat. Her face was lined, solemn, sacred.

There was no ceremony. Not yet.

But in the afternoon, people began to gather.

They came with jars of jam, with bread wrapped in dishtowels, with extra folding chairs and hands that needed to be busy. They set out bowls. They passed mugs. Jack brought coffee in a battered thermos and stood awkwardly near the door. He didn't speak. Just nodded once toward Connor and pressed a stone into his hand.

"Found it near the courthouse steps," he muttered. "Figured she'd want it to stay."

No one corrected him.

Isla arrived later, June clinging shyly to her hand. Phoebe trailed behind, her sweater sleeves too long, chewing nervously at a strand of hair. They brought a pie with a cracked crust and two jars of lake glass. They found space near the back of the room, where the windows let in the light and June could press her nose to the glass.

Near the entryway, Abigail leaned against the doorframe for a long while, eyes swollen but dry. Charlie approached quietly, took her hand, and without a word began helping her arrange shoes by the door. One fell over, and he crouched to fix it.

She pressed her palm to the top of his head, "Thank you," she whispered.

He didn't answer, just stood again, took her hand back to his, and let her lean into him.

It was the kind of love that did not need to be spoken. She had that. Blue had known it too.

As dusk came on, someone lit a fire in the backyard pit. No one claimed the act. One moment the circle was dark, and the next, flames curled into the gray sky like they had always meant to be there.

People sat, scattered, close by, not huddled. Some spoke. Some didn't. Grief moved among them like a wind – circling, skipping, falling still.

Eli arrived just as the light began to fall. He stood at the edge of the trees for a moment, holding a mason jar filled with lake water. He didn't bring it forward. Just held it in his lap when he sat, like an offering. Like a promise.

Later, as the fire flickered lower, Eli stepped inside and into the hallway and froze. The Marantz turntable was still there, needle poised, a record half-sleeved beside it – ready, like she might drop the needle again at any moment.

He reached out, touched the dusted corner of the player. His hand trembled.

He pressed his palm to the wood and dropped to his knees.

She used to dance with him here. Not wild or playful – but close. Chest to chest, cheek to cheek. Her arms wrapped around him in promise. He would never feel that again.

He crumbled forward, silent sobs shaking his back, forehead against the floor. Someone passed in the hallway and paused. Then moved on, giving him space.

There was nothing to fix.

Maggie finally came in from the creek with mud up her shins and a piece of driftwood in her arms. She set it beside the fire. Not for burning. Just to be there.

Abigail passed around candles. She didn't ask anyone to light them. Just pressed them into palms – one for each hand that held her, one for each voice that hummed a lullaby, one for each touch that had said, *You're still here.*

Aviva lit hers without looking up. "Mom?" she said softly, glancing toward Miriam, who sat stiffly in the wicker chair by the window, "Do you want one?"

Miriam didn't answer right away. She reached into her sweater pocket and pulled out something – an old embroidery scrap, frayed at the corners. She held it in her lap, tracing her fingertips over its letters softly.

David stood nearby, silent. Watching Maggie. His mouth twitched – almost a smile. Almost a sob. "She used to sit like that," he said softly, nodding toward Maggie. "By any bit of water she could find. Wouldn't come in for dinner until the frogs started singing."

Miriam looked up, blinking slowly. "She was always collecting things. Stones, feathers, seed pods... her pockets were full of the world."

David nodded, hand pressed to his mouth. "She once told me she was making a map. Not with roads – with feelings." He turned away quickly, but not before Maggie saw the shimmer in his eyes. He didn't say her name, but he whispered, barely audible, "She was ours. Before she ever belonged to the world."

There were no speeches.

But after a while, Caleb lifted his guitar. His fingers shook on the first chord. He paused. Started again. The melody was soft. Familiar. He'd played it once as she glowed beside him, on a quiet shore, when the sun made dust visible and the silence had felt like home.

Amy sang. Her voice was a thread pulled through the dark,

> *We are the fire under rain,*
> *We are the moss on the stones,*
> *We are the hands that still hold,*
> *Even carrying pain*

As they sang, Maggie leaned against Connor's side, watching the sky change. The stars were starting to appear, slowly, like they were remembering themselves. One blinked and then another. The wind shifted.

And somewhere, on the edge of sound, the creek whispered.

Tova placed a flat stone on the table, its surface etched faintly with a word in Hebrew – *Zachor*. Remember.

She lingered by the table a moment longer, her gaze shifting to Miriam and David. "Grief like this," she said softly, not to anyone in particular, "It breaks the natural order." She didn't say more.

She didn't need to.

At the center of it all, a small space remained open. Between the folding chairs, between the hands, between the stories told and the one still held tight in the chest.

HOW TO STAY

A space where something used to be.

A space still warm.

As the fire dimmed, and the candles burned low, a breeze moved through the gathered crowd – soft, briny, familiar. Someone exhaled. Someone else began to weep. Someone laughed under their breath without knowing why.

They did not speak her name.

But the air held it.

In the hush that followed, Maggie whispered to no one in particular, "I think she's still here. Just not in a way you can hold."

And the world, in its quiet, did not disagree.

They stayed until the moon had risen. Until the wax melted. Until the night softened at the edges.

And when they finally rose, one by one, brushing ash from their sleeves and pine needles from their hair, they did not leave her behind. They carried her in soil – stained palms and cedar smoke.

In unfinished songs and in river stones.

In the space between breath and silence.

No one said her name aloud.

They didn't have to.

Blue was there. In breathing. In stillness. In the river of love they had all poured into each other without even knowing.

The light bled from gold to pink, to something deeper – a shade so endless and vast it could only be called blue. And though the sun dipped low, and the stars unfolded one by one, they stayed.

Rooted in the earth.

Buoyed by the river of love she had left behind.

Not mourning a sunset but carrying the color of her onward. Stubborn. Sacred. Alive.

This was not her ending. This was how she stayed.

www.ingramcontent.com/pod-product-compliance
Lightning Source LLC
LaVergne TN
LVHW012025060526
838201LV00061B/4457